PENGUIN CLASSICS
Maigret's Secret

T0248931

'Extraordinary masterpieces ~   ⌐
                                                        – John Banville

'A brilliant writer'   – India Knight

'Intense atmosphere and resonant detail . . . make Simenon's
fiction remarkably like life'   – Julian Barnes

'A truly wonderful writer . . . marvellously readable – lucid,
simple, absolutely in tune with the world he creates'
                                                        – Muriel Spark

'Few writers have ever conveyed with such a sure touch, the
bleakness of human life'   – A. N. Wilson

'Compelling, remorseless, brilliant'   – John Gray

'A writer of genius, one whose simplicity of language creates
indelible images that the florid stylists of our own day can
only dream of'   – *Daily Mail*

'The mysteries of the human personality are revealed in all
their disconcerting complexity'   – Anita Brookner

'One of the greatest writers of our time'   – *The Sunday Times*

'I love reading Simenon. He makes me think of Chekhov'
                                                        – William Faulkner

'One of the great psychological novelists of this century'
                                                        – *Independent*

'The greatest of all, the most genuine novelist we have had
in literature'   – André Gide

'Simenon ought to be spoken of in the same breath as
Camus, Beckett and Kafka'   – *Independent on Sunday*

Georges Simenon was born on 12 February 1903 in Liège, Belgium, and died in 1989 in Lausanne, Switzerland, where he had lived for the latter part of his life. Between 1931 and 1972 he published seventy-five novels and twenty-eight short stories featuring Inspector Maigret.

Simenon always resisted identifying himself with his famous literary character, but acknowledged that they shared an important characteristic:

> My motto, to the extent that I have one, has been noted often enough, and I've always conformed to it. It's the one I've given to old Maigret, who resembles me in certain points . . . 'understand and judge not'.

Penguin is publishing the entire series of Maigret novels.

GEORGES SIMENON

Maigret's Secret

Translated by DAVID WATSON

PENGUIN BOOKS

PENGUIN CLASSICS

UK | USA | Canada | Ireland | Australia
India | New Zealand | South Africa

Penguin Books is part of the Penguin Random House group of companies
whose addresses can be found at global.penguinrandomhouse.com.

First published in French as *Une confidence de Maigret* by Presses de la Cité 1959
This translation first published 2018
002

Set in 12.5/15 pt Dante MT Std
Typeset by Jouve (UK), Milton Keynes
Printed and bound in Great Britain by Clays Ltd, Elcograf S.p.A.

ISBN: 978–0–241–30387–0

www.greenpenguin.co.uk

Contents

1. Madame Pardon's Rice Pudding 1

2. The Geraniums in Rue Caulaincourt 20

3. The Concierge Who Wanted to Get Her Picture in the Paper 40

4. What Adrien Josset Did Next That Night 59

5. Doctor Liorant's Obstinate Silence 79

6. The Old Insomniac 100

7. Monsieur Jules and the Chairwoman 120

8. Madame Maigret's Coq au Vin 142

1. Madame Pardon's Rice Pudding

The maid had just placed the rice pudding in the middle of the round table, and Maigret had to make an effort to look both surprised and delighted as a blushing Madame Pardon cast him a mischievous glance.

It was their umpteenth rice pudding in the four years that the Maigrets had got into the habit of dining at the Pardons' and that the latter had in turn been dining with them a fortnight later at Boulevard Richard-Lenoir, where it was Madame Maigret's turn to lay on a spread.

In the fifth or sixth month of this arrangement, Madame Pardon had served a rice pudding. Maigret had had second and third helpings, saying that the dish reminded him of his childhood and that he hadn't tasted better in the last forty years, which was true.

Since then, every dinner at the Pardons' new apartment in Boulevard Voltaire had been finished off by a helping of the same creamy dessert, which seemed to chime with the cosy, relaxed, slightly dull nature of these occasions.

Neither Maigret nor his wife had family in Paris and they had little experience of regular weekly get-togethers with sisters or sisters-in-law, so the dinners with the Pardons reminded them of visits to see aunts and uncles when they were little.

This evening, the Pardons' daughter, Alice, whom they

had known since she was at school and who had now been married for a year, had joined them along with her husband. She was seven months pregnant and had the 'mask', particularly the red blotches on her nose and under her eyes, and her young husband was paying special attention to what she ate.

Maigret was about to comment once again on how delicious his hostess's rice pudding was when the telephone rang for the third time since they had sat down to eat. They were used to it by now. It had become a sort of joke at the start of the meal to wonder whether the doctor would make it through to dessert without being called by one of his patients.

The telephone sat on a console table surmounted by a mirror. Pardon, with his napkin still in his hand, picked up the receiver.

'Hello! Doctor Pardon here.'

They were watching him in silence and suddenly heard a piercing voice that caused the phone to vibrate. Apart from the doctor, none of them could make out what was being said. It was just a stream of noise, as when you play a record at too fast a speed.

Maigret, however, gave a frown, because he saw his friend's expression turn serious and a worried look pass over his face.

'Yes . . . I'm listening, Madame Kruger . . . Yes . . .'

The woman at the other end of the line didn't need any encouragement to talk. Her words tumbled over each other and, for those who didn't have the receiver next to their ear, formed an incomprehensible but nonetheless pathetic litany.

And there was a drama playing itself out on Pardon's face, mute but expressive. The local doctor, who just a few moments earlier had been smiling, relaxed, joining in the fun of the rice pudding, now seemed a long way from the tranquil bourgeois dining room.

'I understand, Madame Kruger . . . I know, yes . . . If it would be of help, I could come round and . . .'

Madame Pardon looked at the Maigrets as if to say:

'Here we go again! Another dinner we'll have to finish without him . . .'

She was wrong. The voice was still booming out. The doctor was becoming more and more uneasy.

'Yes . . . Of course . . . Try to put them to bed . . .'

They could tell he was feeling despondent, powerless.

'I know . . . I know . . . But I can't do any more than you have . . .'

No one was eating. No one said a word.

'You realize that, if this goes on, it will be you . . .'

He sighed, wiped his brow with his hand. He was forty-five and almost totally bald.

His voice weary, he finally gave another sigh, as if buckling under irresistible pressure:

'Give him one of the pink pills . . . No . . . Just one! . . . Give it half an hour, and if it has had no effect . . .'

Everyone could sense the feeling of relief at the other end of the phone.

'I'll be at home all evening . . . Goodbye, Madame Kruger . . .'

He hung up and came back to the table. They avoided asking him any questions. It took them several minutes to get the conversation flowing again. Pardon remained distracted. The evening followed its usual course. They left the table to have their coffee in the living room, where the table was covered with magazines, as this was the room where his patients waited during surgery hours.

The two windows were open. It was May. The evening was warm, and in spite of the buses and cars there was a hint of spring in the Parisian air. Families from the neighbourhood strolled along Boulevard Voltaire, and there were two men in shirt-sleeves sitting on the café terrace across the road.

When the coffee had been poured, the women picked up their knitting and sat in their usual corner. Pardon and Maigret were seated next to one of the windows, while Alice's young husband, unsure about which group to join, ended up sitting next to his wife.

They had already decided that Madame Maigret would be the godmother, and she was knitting a little jacket for the baby.

Pardon lit a cigar. Maigret filled his pipe. They felt no great compulsion to speak, so they sat there in silence for quite a long time, while listening to the murmur of their wives' conversation.

Finally the doctor muttered, as if to himself:

'Another one of those evenings when I wished I did a different job!'

Maigret didn't press the point or push him into breaking confidences. He liked Pardon a lot. He considered him to be a man, in the fullest sense of the word.

Pardon glanced furtively at his watch.

'It could go on for three or four hours, but she could ring at any moment . . .'

He continued, without providing any details, leaving Maigret to read between the lines:

'A small-time tailor, a Polish Jew, who set up above a herbalist's shop in Rue Popincourt . . . Five children, the eldest nine, and his wife is expecting a sixth . . .'

He gave his daughter's belly an involuntary look when he said this.

'Medical science can do nothing more for him, but five weeks on he is still not dead . . . I've done everything I can to convince him to go into hospital . . . But no sooner do I say the word than he falls into a sort of trance, summons his family to his bedside, cries, groans and begs them not to let anyone take him away against his will . . .'

Pardon was smoking his only cigar of the day without enjoyment.

'They live in two rooms . . . The kids crying all the time . . . His wife's at the end of her tether . . . She's the one I should be tending to, but as long as this goes on I can do nothing . . . I went over there before dinner . . . I gave him an injection and his wife a sedative . . . It isn't having an effect any more . . . While we were eating, he started groaning again, then howling in pain, and his wife, her strength all used up . . .'

Maigret drew on his pipe and muttered:

'I think I understand.'

'Legally, medically, I don't have the right to prescribe him another dose . . . That wasn't the first such telephone call I've received . . . Until now, I've managed to convince her . . .'

He looked at the inspector as if seeking his indulgence.

'Put yourself in my place . . .'

He glanced at his watch again. How much longer would the sick man last out?

The evening was mild, with a certain languor in the air. The murmur of the women's conversation and the rhythmic clack of their needles carried on in the corner of the living room.

Maigret said in a hesitant voice:

'It's not the same, of course . . . but I too have often wished I'd chosen a different profession . . .'

It wasn't a proper, joined-up conversation. It was full of gaps, silences and slow puffs of smoke rising from the inspector's pipe.

'For a while now the police haven't had the powers we enjoyed before, and, by extension, the same responsibilities . . .'

He was thinking out loud. He felt Pardon was a close friend; the feeling was mutual.

'Over the course of my career I have seen our powers gradually diminished in favour of the magistrates. I don't know if that is a good thing or a bad thing. In any case, it's never been our role to pass judgement. It's up to the courts and the juries to decide if a man is guilty or not and to what extent he should be held responsible . . .'

He took it upon himself to do the talking because he sensed that his friend was tense, that his mind was elsewhere, in Rue Popincourt, in the two-room apartment where the Polish tailor was dying.

'Even with the law as it is now, with us as instruments of the prosecutor's office, of the examining magistrate, there still comes a moment when we have to make a decision which will have serious consequences . . . Because, at the end of the day, it is our investigations, the evidence we have gathered, that the magistrates, then the juries, will rely on to form their opinion . . .

'The simple fact of considering a man a suspect, of bringing him into Quai des Orfèvres, of questioning his family, friends, concierge and neighbours about him, can potentially affect the rest of his life . . .'

It was Pardon's turn to murmur:

'I understand.'

'Is such-and-such a person capable of committing a crime? Whatever happens, it is almost always we who ask ourselves the question first. Material evidence is often non-existent, or unconvincing . . .'

The phone rang. Pardon seemed almost afraid to answer, and it was his daughter who picked up the receiver . . .

'Yes, monsieur . . . No, monsieur . . . You have a wrong number . . .'

She explained with a smile:

'Bal des Vertus again . . .'

A dance hall on Rue du Chemin-Vert, whose phone number was very similar to the Pardons'.

Maigret continued, speaking quietly:

'So this apparently normal individual you have before you, was he capable of killing someone or not? Do you see what I'm getting at, Pardon? I'm saying it's not about deciding if he is guilty or not. That's not the business of the Police Judiciaire. But we do have to ask ourselves *if it is possible that* . . . Isn't that a form of judging? I hate that. And if I'd thought about that when I first joined the police, I'm not sure I would have . . .'

A longer silence. He emptied his pipe and took another one from his pocket, which he slowly filled, seeming to caress the briar.

'I remember one case, not so long ago . . . Did you follow the Josset affair?'

'The name rings a bell.'

'There was a lot in the papers about it, but the true story, insofar as there is a true story, was never told.'

It was very unusual for him to talk about a case he had been involved in. Occasionally, at Quai des Orfèvres, among colleagues, some famous case or some difficult investigation might be mentioned, but it was always a passing allusion.

'I recall Josset at the end of his first interrogation, because that's when I had to ask the question . . . I could show you the transcript, so that you can form your own opinion. Only, you would not have had the man himself in front of you for two hours. You wouldn't have heard his voice, seen his facial expressions . . .'

It was at Quai des Orfèvres, in Maigret's office, a Tuesday – he remembered the day – around three o'clock in the afternoon. And it was spring then too – the end of April or the beginning of May.

When he came into work that morning Maigret knew

nothing of the affair, and he wasn't alerted to it until around ten o'clock, firstly by the chief inspector at Auteuil and subsequently by Examining Magistrate Coméliau.

There was some confusion that day. The inspector from Auteuil claimed that he had informed the Police Judiciaire in the early hours of the morning, but for some reason the message did not seem to have reached its destination.

So it was nearly eleven o'clock before Maigret took a car to Rue Lopert, two or three hundred metres from the church at Auteuil, and found that he was the last to arrive. The reporters and photographers were already there, along with a hundred or so curious onlookers, being held back by uniformed policemen. The men from the prosecutor's office were already on the scene, and five minutes later Criminal Records showed up.

At 12.10 Maigret showed into his office one Adrien Josset, a handsome, still quite lean forty-year-old, who cut an elegant figure despite his unshaven, crumpled appearance.

'Come in, please . . . Take a seat.'

He opened the door of the inspectors' room and summoned young Lapointe.

'Bring a pad and pencil . . .'

The office was bathed in sunlight, and the noises of Paris could be heard through the open window. Lapointe understood that he was required to take a shorthand record of the interrogation and sat down at the corner of the table. Maigret filled his pipe and watched a convoy of boats going up the Seine and a man in a barge allowing his vessel to drift.

'Forgive me, Monsieur Josset, but I am obliged to record

the answers you will be so kind as to give to my questions . . . I hope you aren't too tired.'

The man shook his head with a vaguely bitter smile. He hadn't slept a wink all night, and the police at Auteuil had already subjected him to a long interrogation.

Maigret hadn't wanted to read it, preferring instead to form his own impression.

'To begin with the boring formalities . . . Could you tell me your surname, first names, age, profession . . . ?'

'Adrien Josset, forty, born Sète, Hérault . . .'

It was only when he said that that Maigret picked up the slight hint of a southern accent.

'Your father?'

'Schoolteacher. He died ten years ago.'

'Is your mother still alive?'

'Yes. She still lives in the same little house in Sète.'

'Did you study in Paris?'

'Montpellier.'

'You are a pharmacist, I believe.'

'I trained in pharmacy, then did one year of medicine. I didn't follow through on that.'

'Why not?'

He hesitated, and Maigret could see it was out of a kind of honesty. It was clear that he was trying hard to give accurate, truthful replies, so far at least.

'For different reasons, probably. But the main one was that I had a girlfriend who went with her parents to Paris.'

'Did she become your wife?'

'No. As a matter of fact, our relationship broke down a few months later . . . But I think my heart wasn't in being a doctor . . . My parents weren't well off . . . they had to make sacrifices to pay for my studies . . . Even if I'd qualified as a doctor, I'd have found it hard to set up in practice . . .'

He was so tired he was struggling to string his thoughts together, and he cast the occasional glance at Maigret as if to check that he was making a favourable impression on the inspector.

'Is this important?'

'Anything might be important.'

'I understand . . . I wondered whether I had any particular vocation . . . I'd heard about career opportunities in laboratories . . . Most pharmaceutical companies have their own research laboratories . . . When I got to Paris with my pharmacy diploma in my pocket I tried to find one of these jobs . . .'

'Without success?'

'All I could find was a job as a temporary stand-in at a chemist's, then another . . .'

He was feeling hot. So was Maigret, who was now pacing up and down in the room, pausing occasionally by the window.

'Did they ask you all these questions at Auteuil?'

'No. Not the same questions. I can see that you are attempting to understand who I am. As you see, I'm trying hard to give you honest answers. Deep down, I see myself as no better or no worse than anyone else . . .'

He had to wipe his brow.

'Are you thirsty?'

'A bit . . .'

Maigret opened the door to the inspectors' room.

'Janvier? Could you get us something to drink?'

Then, to Josset:

'Beer?'

'If you like.'

'Are you hungry?'

Without waiting for a reply he turned again to Janvier:

'Beer and sandwiches.'

Josset gave a sad smile.

'I read about that . . .' he murmured.

'You read what?'

'Beer, sandwiches. The chief and his inspectors taking it in turns to ask questions. It's common knowledge, isn't it? I never thought that one day . . .'

He had fine hands and he sometimes wrung them nervously.

'You know when you get here, but . . .'

'Don't be alarmed, Monsieur Josset. I can promise you that I have no preconceived ideas about you . . .'

'The inspector at Auteuil certainly did.'

'Was he rough with you?'

'He didn't treat me well. He used some words which . . . Anyway, who knows? If I were him . . .'

'Let's get back to those early days in Paris. How long was it before you met the woman who would become your wife?'

'About a year . . . I was twenty-five and working in an English chemist's on Faubourg Saint-Honoré when I met her . . .'

'Was she a customer?'

'Yes.'

'What was her maiden name?'

'Fontane, Christine Fontane. But she was still using the name of her first husband, who had died a few months earlier – Lowell – from the English brewing family. You'll have seen the name on beer bottles.'

'So she had been a widow for a few months and she was . . . what age?'

'Twenty-nine.'

'Any children?'

'No.'

'Rich?'

'Indeed. She was a regular customer of all the luxury shops on Faubourg Saint-Honoré . . .'

'Did you become her lover?'

'She had a free and easy lifestyle.'

'Even when her husband was alive?'

'I believe that was the case.'

'What was her background?'

'Bourgeois . . . Not wealthy, but comfortably well off . . . She grew up in the sixteenth arrondissement, and her father was chair on a number of company boards . . .'

'Did you fall in love with her?'

'Head over heels.'

'Had you already split up with your girlfriend from Montpellier?'

'Several months earlier.'

'Did you and Christine Lowell discuss the prospect of marriage from the very start?'

The briefest of hesitations.

'No.'

There was a knock at the door. It was the waiter from the Brasserie Dauphine, bringing some beer and sandwiches. This gave them an excuse to take a break. Josset didn't eat but merely drank half of his beer, while Maigret continued to pace up and down, nibbling on a sandwich.

'Can you tell me how it happened?'

'I will try. It's not easy. Fifteen years have passed. I was young, I can see that now. With hindsight, life was different then. Certain things didn't seem as important as they do now.

'I wasn't earning a lot of money. I was living in furnished lodgings, near Place des Ternes, and I had all my meals in cheap restaurants, except when I would make do with some croissants. I spent more money on clothes than I did on feeding myself . . .'

He still had a taste for fashion: the suit he was wearing was by one of the finest tailors in Paris; his monogrammed shirt had been made to measure, as had his shoes.

'Christine lived in a different world, which I knew nothing about and which dazzled me. I was still the son of a small-town schoolteacher, and the students I mixed with in Montpellier weren't much better off than me.'

'Did she introduce you to her friends?'

'Much later. That was an aspect to our relationship that took me a long time to figure out.'

'Can you give me an example?'

'We often hear about businessmen, industrialists or bankers having a fling with a shopgirl or a model. It was much the same for her, in reverse. She was dating an inexperienced, penniless pharmacist's assistant. She insisted on knowing where I lived, a cheap furnished hotel with earthenware tiles on the walls of the stairwell, and walls so thin you could hear every noise. It delighted her. On Sundays she would take me out in the car to some country inn.'

His voice had become muted, tinged with both sadness and resentment.

'In the beginning I too thought it was just a fling that wouldn't last.'

'Were you in love?'

'I grew to love her.'

'Were you jealous?'

'That's how it all began. She would speak to me about her friends and even her lovers. She enjoyed telling me all the details. At first I didn't say anything. Then, in a fit of jealousy, I called her every name under the sun and ended up giving her a slap. I was convinced she was making fun of me and that once she left my iron bed she gossiped to everyone about how awkward and naive I was. We had lots of arguments along those lines. I once stopped seeing her for a month.'

'Was she the one who patched things up?'

'Her or me. Either one of us might ask for forgiveness. We really did love each other, inspector.'

'Who first raised the question of marriage?'

'I can't recall. To be honest, it's impossible to say. We reached the point where we were hurting each other deliberately. Sometimes she'd turn up at three in the morning, half drunk, and knock on the door of my room. If I was in a sulk and didn't answer straight away the

15

neighbours would be up in arms about the racket. I don't know how many times she threatened to kick me out. They did at the chemist's too, because some mornings I'd turn up late, still half asleep.'

'Did she drink a lot?'

'We both drank. I don't really know why. We just did it without thinking. It made us even more exhilarated. In the end we realized that I couldn't do without her, and she couldn't do without me.'

'Where was she living at this time?'

'In the house you saw, in Rue Lopert. It was around two or three in the morning one night, we were sitting in a cabaret bar when we looked each other in the eye and, suddenly sobered up, asked ourselves in earnest where we were going.'

'You don't know who first raised it?'

'No, in all honesty. It was the first time the word "marriage" was mentioned, and on that occasion it was just a throwaway remark, more or less. It's hard to say after all this time.'

'She was five years older than you?'

'Yes, and a few million francs better off than me. Once we were married I couldn't go on working behind the counter in a chemist's. She knew someone called Virieu, who had inherited a modest pharmaceutical concern from his parents. Virieu wasn't a pharmacist. He was thirty-five but had spent most of his adult life in Fouquet's, Maxim's and the casino in Deauville. Christine invested some money in his company, and I became the managing director.'

'So in fact you finally achieved your ambition?'

'It appears that way, I admit. When you look at the sequence of events, it's as if I carefully planned each stage. However, I assure you that was very far from the case.

'I married Christine because I loved her passionately and because if I'd had to do without her I'd probably have killed myself. For her part, she begged me to make our union legal.

'For a long time afterwards she had no more affairs and began to be jealous herself; she came to hate my customers and would drop by to check up on me.

'An opportunity came along to provide me with a position in keeping with her lifestyle. The money she invested in the business was in her name, and the marriage followed the convention of separate assets.

'Some people saw me as a gigolo, and I wasn't always accepted with open arms in this new milieu in which I was to lead my life.'

'Were you happy together?'

'I suppose so. I worked hard. I took on this relatively obscure laboratory and turned it into one of the four major centres in Paris. We socialized a lot too, so you could say I didn't have a spare moment, day or night.'

'Don't you want to eat?'

'I'm not hungry. If you don't mind, I'll have another glass of beer.'

'Were you drunk last night?'

'That's what they asked me this morning. Doubtless I was at one point, but I still remember everything.'

'I didn't want to read the statement you made at Auteuil, which I have here.'

Maigret idly flicked through the pages.

'Is there anything there you would like to change?'

'I told the truth. Maybe I overdid it, because of the inspector's attitude. From his opening questions I realized that he regarded me as a murderer. Later on, when the prosecutor's men turned up in Rue Lopert, I got the impression that the magistrate shared that opinion.'

He was silent for a few moments.

'I can understand that. I was wrong to get worked up about it.'

Maigret asked blandly:

'So you didn't kill your wife?'

And Josset shook his head. He was no longer protesting vehemently. He looked weary, deflated.

'I know it will be difficult to explain . . .'

'Would you like to take a break?'

The man hesitated. He rocked gently on his chair.

'I think it would be better to go on. But would you allow me to get up and walk around a bit?'

He too wanted to go to the window, to see the city outside going about its everyday business in the sunlight.

The previous evening he was still part of it. Maigret followed him with his eyes, lost in thought. Lapointe sat with his pencil poised in his hand.

Back in the peaceful living room in Boulevard Voltaire – a little too peaceful, in fact, almost oppressively calm – where the women were still knitting and chatting, Doctor Pardon listened carefully to Maigret's every word.

Maigret, however, could sense that there was still an

invisible link between his listener and the telephone on the console table, between the doctor and the Polish tailor who was fighting his last battle alongside his five children and his hysterical wife.

A bus went by, stopped and then set off again, having deposited two dark figures, and a drunk bumped along the walls without ever interrupting the tune he was humming.

2. *The Geraniums in Rue Caulaincourt*

'Heavens!' Alice cried suddenly as she bounded to her feet. 'I forgot the liqueurs!'

She had changed quite a lot. When she was a young girl, she rarely attended these dinners; she must have found them boring. She wasn't much in evidence in the first few months of her marriage either, maybe one or two appearances, to show off her new role as wife, on a par, so to speak, with her mother.

But since she had been expecting, she had paid frequent visits to Boulevard Voltaire, where she happily assumed the role of hostess and suddenly started to take an even closer interest than her mother in the minutiae of housework.

Her husband, a newly qualified veterinarian, leaped up from his seat, made his wife sit down again and went into the kitchen in search of some brandy for the men and, for the women, that Dutch liqueur that was no longer found anywhere except at the Pardons' house.

Like most doctors' waiting rooms, this one was badly lit, and the furniture was worn and shabby. Maigret and Pardon, sitting by the open window, had a good view of the glaring streetlights on the boulevard, where the leaves of the trees were starting to rustle. Was there a storm on the way?

'Brandy, inspector?'

Maigret smiled at the young man distractedly; though

he was well aware of where he was, his thoughts nonetheless were back in his office, bathed in sunshine, on that memorable Tuesday when the interrogation took place.

He had more on his mind than at dinner, his mood matching the doctor's serious demeanour. He and Pardon could almost read each other's thoughts, even though they had got to know each other late in life, and both were well advanced in their respective careers. They had hit it off from the start, and soon a strong mutual respect had developed between them.

Perhaps this was due to the fact that they applied the same standards of honesty, not just towards other people but also towards themselves. They didn't play games, they didn't sugar the pill, they both called a spade a spade.

This evening, when Maigret suddenly began to hold forth, it was less to distract his friend than because the telephone call had reawakened in him similar feelings to those that were currently exercising Pardon.

It wasn't that he had a guilt complex – he hated that expression anyway. Nor was it that he felt remorse.

Both of them, because of their profession, a profession they had been drawn to, sometimes found themselves in a situation where they had to make a choice, and that choice had implications for someone else's fate: in Pardon's case, whether a man lived or died.

Neither of them romanticized this responsibility. Neither was oppressed by it or rebelled against it. They simply treated it with a certain melancholy seriousness.

Young Bruart wasn't sure he could sit near them. He would have liked to know what they were whispering about and was aware that he was still an outsider in this little clan. So he went back to sit with the women.

'There were three of us in my office,' said Maigret. 'Lapointe, who was recording the interview and casting me the occasional glance, Adrien Josset, who was sometimes on his feet, sometimes sitting in his chair, and me, mainly sitting with my back to the open window.

'I realized how tired the man was. He hadn't slept a wink. He had had a lot to drink, firstly the previous evening, then again in the middle of the night. I could sense the waves of exhaustion washing over him; sometimes he seemed a bit dizzy. Sometimes his worried eyes became fixed and expressionless, as if, sinking into a torpor, he was trying to struggle back to the surface.

'It may seem cruel to have pushed on with this first interrogation: it would end up lasting more than three hours.

'However, it was as much for his sake as out of a sense of duty that I stuck to the task. For one thing, I couldn't pass up the opportunity to extract a confession, if there was one to be had. And besides, short of giving him an injection or a sedative, he would not have been able to rest anyway, given that his nerves were shot.

'He needed to talk, to talk there and then. If I'd sent him off to the cells, he'd have sat there talking to himself.

'The reporters and photographers had gathered in the corridor. I could hear their loud voices and laughter.

'It was around then that the afternoon papers came out, and I was sure that they must be talking about the crime at Auteuil, and that the photos of Josset taken that morning in Rue Lopert must be plastered all over their front pages.

'It wasn't long before I got a telephone call from Examining Magistrate Coméliau, who was always anxious to get an early result in the cases under his jurisdiction.

'"Have you got Josset there with you?"

'"Yes."

'"Has he confessed?"

'Josset was looking at me, aware we were talking about him.

'"I'm quite busy," I said, without being specific.

'"Is he denying it?"

'"I don't know."

'"Make it clear to him that it would be in his best interests to—"

'"I'll try."

'Coméliau is not a bad man, but he has been called my friendly enemy, because we have clashed so often.

'It's not really his fault. It springs from how he sees his role, hence his duty. In his view, he is paid to defend society, so he has to show no mercy to anything that threatens to upset the established order. I don't think that he has ever experienced a moment of self-doubt. He has no compunction in distinguishing the good people from the bad people and seems incapable of conceiving that people can exist in the grey area in between.

'If I'd told him that I hadn't formed an opinion yet, he wouldn't have believed me or he would have accused me of being dilatory in the exercise of my duties.

'Nevertheless, after an hour, two hours of interrogation I was no nearer to answering the question that Josset asked whenever he looked at me with his wide eyes: *You do believe me, don't you?*

'The previous evening, I didn't even know him. I'd never heard anyone talk about him. His name was vaguely familiar to me, but that was only because I had used medicine from a box with the name "Josset and Virieu" on it.

'Oddly, I had never even set foot in Rue Lopert before, so I had discovered its existence that morning with some surprise.

'There isn't usually much crime in the area around the Auteuil church. And Rue Lopert, which is a cul-de-sac, more a private lane than a proper street, has only about twenty houses, of the sort you might find in a provincial village.

'It's only a short hop from Rue Chardon-Lagache, and yet you feel a long way from the bustle of Paris. The names of the neighbouring streets commemorate writers rather than great statesmen: Rue Boileau, Rue Théophile-Gautier, Rue Leconte-de-Lisle . . .

'I wanted to go back to the house, which stood out from the others in the street. It was made almost entirely of glass and had odd, unexpected angles. It was built around 1925 in the Decorative Arts period.

'It was all new to me: the décor, the colours, the furniture, the layout of the rooms. It perplexed me how people lived their lives there.

'The man in front of me, fighting against exhaustion and a hangover, kept on asking with his anxious but resigned gaze: *You do believe me, don't you?*

'The inspector at Auteuil hadn't believed him and had shown him no consideration.

'At one point I had opened the door to tell the reporters to shut up, as they were making so much noise . . .'

For the second or third time Josset refused the sandwich that was offered to him. It was as if he felt his strength might fail him at any moment and he was determined to see this through at any cost.

And perhaps it wasn't only that he had a divisional detective chief inspector before him, someone who could have a big influence in what happened to him.

He needed to convince someone, anyone, a man other than himself.

'Were you happy, you and your wife?'

How would Maigret or Pardon have answered that question? Josset also hesitated.

'I think there were times when we were happy. Especially when we were alone together. Especially at night. We were true lovers. Do you understand what I'm saying? And if we had been able to be on our own more often . . .'

He would have been more explicit if he could!

'I don't know how familiar you are with this world. I wasn't at all before I found my way in. Christine had grown up in it. She needed it. She had lots of friends. A packed diary. If she was ever alone for a moment she'd be on the telephone. There were lunches, cocktail parties, dinners, dress rehearsals, cabaret suppers. There were hundreds of people with whom we were on first-name terms and whom we'd bump into at all these venues.

'She loved me once, I'm sure of that. And in a sense she probably still did love me.'

'What about you?' Maigret asked.

'I loved her too. No one will believe me. Even our friends, who know all about it, will say otherwise. Nevertheless, we were united by something stronger than conventional love.

'We weren't lovers any more, except on rare occasions.'

'How long had this been going on?'

'A few years. Four or five. I can't say exactly. I couldn't even tell you how we got that way.'

'Did you argue?'

'Yes and no. It depends what you mean by "argue". We knew each other so well. We had no illusions about each other, it was impossible to cheat. In the end we were merciless.'

'Merciless about what?'

'All the little faults, the tiny acts of cowardice that are part of everyone. In the beginning you turn a blind eye or, if you notice them, you try to turn them into something appealing.'

'You transform them into qualities?'

'Let's just say that your partner becomes more human, more vulnerable, which makes you want to protect them and smother them with tenderness. You see, I'm sure that the fundamental thing was that I wasn't at all prepared for this life.

'Do you know our offices in Avenue Marceau? We also have laboratories in Saint-Mandé, and in Switzerland and Belgium. That was, and indeed still is, a part of my life, the most solid part. You asked me just now if I was happy. When I was there, managing an ever-expanding company, I felt fulfilled. Then, suddenly, the phone would ring. Christine would want to meet me somewhere.'

'Did you feel, because of her money, that you were subordinate to her?'

'I don't think so. Some people thought, and probably still do, that it was a marriage based on money.'

'Is that incorrect? Money wasn't a factor at all?'

'I swear.'

'The business remained in your wife's name?'

'Unfortunately not. She retained a large share, but an almost equal-sized part was signed over to me six years ago.'

'At your request?'

'At Christine's. I'd like to point out that, as far as she was concerned, this wasn't a recognition of the results of my hard work but rather a scheme to avoid certain taxes without ceding shares to third parties. But I know I can't prove it and it will count against me. Along with the fact that Christine drew up a new will in my favour. I haven't read it. I haven't seen it. I don't even know where it is. She told me about it one evening when she was depressed and thought that she had cancer.'

'Was she in good health?'

He hesitated, still giving the impression that he was scrupulously weighing up his words and their exact meanings.

'She didn't have cancer or heart disease or any of those ailments that you read about in the papers every week and for which they collect money in the street. But in my view she was nonetheless very ill. Recently, she did not experience more than a few hours of lucidity each day, and sometimes she locked herself away in her bedroom for two or three days at a time.'

'You don't share a bedroom?'

'We did for several years. But then, because I got up early in the morning and was waking her up, I moved into the adjoining room.'

'Did she drink heavily?'

'If you question her friends, as I'm sure you will, they will tell you that she didn't drink more than many of them. They only saw her in her best light, if you follow me. They didn't know that before going out for two or three hours she would spend several hours in bed and that, the next day, as soon as she woke up, she'd be back on the booze or on pills.'

'Do you drink?'

Josset shrugged, as if to say that Maigret only had to look at him to get his answer.

'Less than her, anyway. Not as obsessively. Otherwise the laboratories would have gone down the pan years ago. But I do sometimes get drunk and act like someone who has had one too many, so you will find that these same friends will tell you I was more of a soak than she was. Especially as I can sometimes get aggressive when I'm drunk. If you haven't been in the same situation, how would you understand?'

'I'm trying to,' Maigret sighed.

Then he asked point-blank:

'Do you have a mistress?'

'Here we go! They asked me that this morning and when I replied the inspector looked triumphant, as if he had finally nailed the truth.'

'How long?'

'A year.'

'So a long time after your relationship with your wife began to break down, which happened, I think you said, five or six years ago?'

'A long time after, yes, and completely unrelated. Before that I had had a few affairs, like everyone, most of them just short flings.'

'Whereas you are in love with your current mistress?'

'I don't like to use the same word that I used for Christine, because it's something very different. But how can I put it?'

'Who is she?'

'My secretary. When I told the other inspector, he must have been expecting it, because he was immensely pleased with himself that he had seen my answer coming. Let's face it, it's so banal it's the subject of jokes. And yet . . .'

The beer glasses were empty. Most of the passers-by they had seen earlier on the bridge and the quayside had now been absorbed by the offices and shops, where work had resumed.

'Her name is Annette Duché. She is twenty years old, and her father is head clerk at the sub-préfecture at Fontenay-le-Comte. He is in Paris currently, and I'd be very surprised if he doesn't come to see you once the newspapers appear.'

'To accuse you?'

'Perhaps. I don't know. When something happens, when a person dies under mysterious circumstances, everything becomes complicated all of a sudden. Do you see what I'm trying to say? Nothing is normal and obvious any more, nothing just happens by chance. Every action and word takes on a damning meaning. I'm quite aware of what I'm saying, I promise you. I may need a bit of time to get my thoughts in order, but from now on I really want you to know that I'm not hiding anything from you and will do my utmost to help you to uncover the truth . . .

'Annette worked at Avenue Marceau for six months before I even noticed her, because Monsieur Jules, the head of personnel, put her in shipping, which is on another floor from my office, and I rarely set foot there. One afternoon, when my secretary was off sick and I had an important report to dictate, they sent her to me. We worked until eleven at night in the empty building, and as I felt guilty that I had made her miss her dinner I took her for a bite to eat in a local restaurant.

'That's pretty much it. I've just turned forty, and she is twenty. She reminds me of some of the girls I knew in Sète and Montpellier. I didn't make a move for a long time. At first I had her transferred into an office next to mine, where I was able to observe her. I found out things about her. I heard that she was a sensible girl, that to begin with she had lived with an aunt in Rue Lamarck, but then she had fallen out with her and moved out to a rented room in Rue Caulaincourt.

'I know this sounds ridiculous, but I even walked round to Rue Caulaincourt and saw the pots of geraniums on her window-sill on the fourth floor.

'Nothing happened for about three months. Then, when we set up a branch office in Brussels, I sent my secretary there and installed Annette in her place . . .'

'Was your wife aware of all this?'

'We didn't hide anything from each other.'

'Did she have lovers?'

'If I answer that people will make out that I'm trying to blacken her name in order to defend myself. The dead are sacrosanct.'

'How did she react?'

'Christine? She didn't react at first. She just gave me a vaguely pitying look.

'"Poor Adrien! Has it come to this?"

'She would ask for updates on "the little girl", as she called her.

'"Isn't she pregnant yet? What will you do when it happens? Will you ask for a divorce?"'

Maigret frowned and observed the other man a little more closely.

'Is Annette pregnant?' he asked.

'No! That, at least, can be proved easily.'

'Is she still living in Rue Caulaincourt?'

'She hasn't changed her lifestyle at all. I didn't provide her with an apartment, I didn't buy her a car or jewels or a fur coat. The geraniums are still there on her windowsill. In her room she has a glass-fronted walnut wardrobe like the one my parents had and she still uses the kitchen as her dining room.'

His bottom lip was trembling, as if he were issuing a challenge.

'You didn't want to change it?'

'No.'

'Did you often spend the night at Rue Caulaincourt?'

'Once or twice a week.'

'Can you give me as accurate an account as possible of what you were doing yesterday in the daytime and at night?'

'Where do you want me to begin?'

'The morning.'

Maigret turned to Lapointe as if to indicate that he should take all this down.

'I got up at seven thirty, as usual, and I went out on to the terrace to do my morning exercises.'

'So you were in Rue Lopert?'

'Yes.'

'What had you been doing the previous evening?'

'Christine and I went to the première of *Witnesses* at the Théâtre de la Madeleine, and we had supper afterwards in a cabaret in Place Pigalle.'

'Did you have an argument?'

'No. I had a busy day ahead of me. We were considering changing the packaging on some of our products; good presentation can make an enormous difference to sales.'

'What time did you get to bed?'

'Around two o'clock in the morning.'

'Did your wife go to bed at the same time?'

'No. I left her in Montmartre with some friends we had met up with.'

'Their names?'

'The Joublins. Gaston Joublin is a lawyer. They live in Rue Washington.'

'Do you know what time your wife got home?'

'No. I was fast asleep.'

'Had you been drinking?'

'A few glasses of champagne. I was fully compos mentis; my mind was on my work the next day.'

'Did you go into your wife's room in the morning?'

'I peeked round the door and saw that she was still asleep.'

'You didn't wake her up?'

'No.'

'Why did you open the door?'

'Just to make sure she had got home.'

'Did she sometimes not come home?'

'Occasionally.'

'Was she alone?'

'As far as I know, she has never brought anyone home.'

'How many servants do you have?'

'Not very many for a house of our size. Of course, we rarely ate at home. The cook, Madame Siran, who is more like what the English call a housekeeper, doesn't spend the night at Rue Lopert but lives with her son in the Javel quarter, on the other side of Pont Mirabeau. He is around thirty, single, in poor health and works for the Métro.

'The only one in residence is the chambermaid, a Spanish woman called Carlotta . . .'

'Who makes your breakfast?'

'Carlotta. Madame Siran doesn't arrive until just before I set off.'

'So did everything happen as normal yesterday morning?'

'Yes . . . I'm thinking . . . No, nothing out of the ordinary . . . I had my bath, got dressed, went downstairs to eat, and when I got into my car, which I leave parked outside the front door at night, I noticed Madame Siran coming round the corner, her shopping basket in her hand, because she does her shopping on the way here.'

'Do you have just the one car?'

'Two. The one I use is an English two-seater, because I have a passion for sports cars. Christine drives an American car.'

'Was your wife's car parked by the pavement?'

'Yes. Rue Lopert is a quiet street, not much traffic, very easy to park there.'

'Did you go straight to Avenue Marceau?'

'No! And I know this will be used against me too. I went to Rue Caulaincourt to pick up Annette.'

'Do you go there every morning?'

'More or less. I have a retractable roof. In spring it's a real pleasure driving through Paris early in the morning.'

'Did you turn up at work with your secretary?'

'For a long time I dropped her off at the nearest Métro station. Some people from work saw us. So everyone knew in the end, and I decided to be up-front about it. Indeed, I think I derived a certain pleasure from being so open, defying public opinion, as it were. You see, I detest all the smirks, the whispering behind your back, the knowing looks. Since there was nothing inappropriate about our relationship, I didn't see why . . .'

He was hoping for approval, but Maigret remained impassive. That was his role.

It was a lovely spring morning, as on the day before, and the little sports car drove down from Montmartre and threaded its way through the traffic, skirting the gold-tipped railings at the edge of Parc Monceau, crossing Place des Ternes, circling the Arc de Triomphe, at an hour when the crowds looked fresh and ready for the new day as they hurried to work.

'I spent the morning in discussions with my departmental heads, especially the sales director.'

'Was Annette present?'

'Her desk is in my office.'

Which would have tall windows, no doubt, and overlook the elegant avenue, where expensive cars would be parked along the pavements.

'Did you have lunch with her?'

'No. I took an important English client who had just arrived to lunch at the Berkeley.'

'Did you receive any word from your wife?'

'I rang her at two thirty, when I got back to the office.'

'Was she awake?'

'She was just getting up. She told me that she was going to do some shopping and then would be dining with a girlfriend.'

'Did she mention a name?'

'I don't think so. I would have remembered. It was something she did a lot, so I didn't pay it much attention. I returned to the meeting, which had broken up for lunch.'

'Did anything out of the ordinary happen that afternoon?'

'Not out of the ordinary, but important nonetheless. Around four o'clock I sent one of our errand boys to a shop in the Madeleine to buy some hors d'œuvres – a lobster, some Russian salad and some fruit. I told him, if the first cherries had arrived, to buy two punnets. He put all the shopping in my car. At six o'clock, my colleagues went home, as did most of the staff. At six fifteen Monsieur Jules, the firm's most senior employee, popped in to see if I needed him any more, then went off in turn.'

'What about your partner, Monsieur Virieu?'

'He had already left around five o'clock. In spite of his experience, he is a bit of an amateur and his role is largely as the face of the firm. He is the one who usually invites our foreign associates and major clients out to lunch or dinner.'

'Was he at the lunch with the Englishman?'

'Yes. He also goes to conferences.'

'So you and your secretary were alone in the building?'

'Apart from the concierge, obviously. It happens quite often. We left, and once we were in the car I decided to make the most of the good weather to go for an aperitif out of town. Driving relaxes me. We soon got to the Chevreuse valley and had a drink in an inn.'

'Did you and Annette ever eat out in a restaurant?'

'Rarely. At first I avoided it because I wanted to keep our relationship more or less secret. Later, I simply grew fond of our little dinners in her apartment in Rue Caulaincourt.'

'With the geraniums in the window?'

Josset looked offended.

'You find that amusing?' he said with a hint of aggression.

'No.'

'Don't you get it?'

'I believe I do.'

'Even the lobster should give you a clue. In my family, when I was a child, we only ever ate lobster on big occasions. It was the same in Annette's family. When we had our little dinners, as we called them, we looked for dishes that we used to crave during our youth. In fact, I bought her a present in the same spirit: a refrigerator, which hums away in the corner of her not-very-modern apartment and allows us to chill a bottle of white wine, or sometimes open a bottle of champagne. Are you laughing at me?'

Maigret shook his head to reassure him. It was Lapointe who gave a smile, as if this brought to mind some recent memories.

'It was just before eight when we arrived at Rue Caulaincourt. There's one thing I should add in passing. The concierge, who was quite motherly towards Annette in the beginning, before I'd set foot in the building, later took a dislike to her. She would mutter offensive words at her when she came in and would turn her back completely on me. We passed in front of the lodge where she and her family were at the dinner table, and I could have sworn that woman looked at us with an evil smile.

'It made enough of an impression that I wanted to turn round and ask her what she had to be so happy about.

'I didn't, but we would find out only half an hour later. Upstairs, I took my jacket off and laid the table while Annette got changed. I make no secret of it. That's also part of the pleasure, it helps me feel young again. She spoke to me from the next room, while I cast the occasional glance through the half-open door. Her body is so young, so smooth, so easy on the eye.

'I suppose all this will be trawled over in public. Unless I can find someone who believes me . . .'

He closed his eyes with tiredness, and Maigret went to get him a glass of water from the cupboard, deciding not to give him some cognac from the bottle he always kept in reserve.

It was too soon for that. He feared it might wind him up too much.

'Just as we sat down to eat in front of the open window Annette thought she heard something, and a little later I heard it too: some footsteps on the stairs. There was nothing surprising in that, as the building has five floors, and there are three apartments above our heads.

'Why did she feel embarrassed all of a sudden to be sitting there dressed only in a blue satin dressing gown? The footsteps stopped on our floor. There was a knock on the door, and a voice said: "I know you're in there. Open the door!"

'It was her father. In the time we had known each other, Annette and I, he had never come to Paris. I had never seen him. She had described him to me as a sad man, severe and withdrawn. A widower for some years, he lived alone, closed in on himself, with no interests in life.

'"Just a moment, Papa! . . ."

'There wasn't enough time to get dressed again. I didn't think of putting my jacket back on. She opened the door. He looked at me first of all, his eyes hard under his bushy grey eyebrows.

'"Your employer?" he asked his daughter.

'"Monsieur Josset, yes . . ."

'His gaze drifted to the table and landed on the red slash of the lobster, the bottle of Riesling.

'"It's just as they said," he muttered as he sat down in a chair.

'He hadn't taken his hat off. He sized me up, pursing his lips in disgust.

'"I suppose you keep your pyjamas and slippers in the wardrobe?"

'What he said was true, and I blushed. If he had gone into the bathroom he would have found a razor, a shaving brush, my toothbrush and my usual choice of toothpaste.

'Annette hadn't dared to look at him at first. Now she merely observed him and noticed that he was breathing in a strange way, as if the climb up the stairs had left him out of breath. Also, his body was swaying oddly.

'"Have you been drinking, Papa?" she cried.

'He never drank. Probably he had already come to Rue Caulaincourt during the day and spoken to the concierge. Perhaps she had written to him to put him in the picture.

'Then, while he waited, had he perhaps installed himself in the little bar opposite, from where he had seen us enter the building?

'He had drunk to build up his courage. His complexion was grey, his clothes were loose-fitting, as if he had once been a big man, perhaps even a jovial one.

'"So, it's true, then . . ."

'He looked at us both in turn, searching for the right words, probably just as ill at ease as we were.

'Finally he turned to me and asked in a tone that was both threatening and ashamed at the same time:

'"What are you planning to do?"'

3. The Concierge Who Wanted to Get Her Picture in the Paper

Maigret condensed this part of the interrogation into twenty or thirty replies that seemed to him the most salient. He rarely spoke continuously. His conversations with Doctor Pardon were punctuated with silences, in which he drew slowly on his pipe, as if allowing the content of his next sentence time to take shape. He knew that his words had the same meaning for his friend, the same resonances as they did for him.

'A situation so banal it is the stuff of hackneyed jokes. There are probably tens of thousands of men in Paris alone in the same circumstances. For the vast majority it all works out more or less well in the end. The drama, if there is any, takes place at home and involves a separation, sometimes a divorce, then life goes on . . .'

The man before him in his office, which smelled of spring and of tobacco, was battling for his survival and from time to time he looked at the inspector to see whether he still had a fighting chance.

The three-handed scene in the lodgings in Rue Caulaincourt had been both dramatic and sordid. It is that very mixture of sincerity and comedy, of the tragic and the grotesque, that is so hard to express, so hard even to visualize, after the event, and Maigret understood Josset's dismay as he searched for the right words but never managed to find them.

'I'm sure, inspector, that Annette's father is an honest man. And yet! . . . He doesn't drink, I've already told you that. He has been living an austere existence since his wife died. He seems like a man who is consumed by something . . . I don't know . . . It's just a guess . . . Perhaps it is remorse that he didn't make her happier?

'But yesterday, as he waited for us to turn up in Rue Caulaincourt, he had had several drinks. He had found himself in a bar, the only place from which he could keep an eye on the building, and had ordered a drink without thinking, or for Dutch courage, and then just unwittingly carried on drinking . . .

'When he stood in front of me, he hadn't lost control of himself, but it wouldn't have been possible to hold a coherent conversation with him.

'What could I say in reply to his question?

'He stared at me with that same serious look and repeated it:

'"What are you planning to do?"

'And I, who had a clear conscience just a few moments earlier, who was so proud of our love that I couldn't resist the desire to show it to the world, now suddenly felt guilty.

'We had barely started to eat. I can still picture the red of the lobster and the red of the geraniums, Annette clutching her blue dressing gown over her chest and holding back her tears.

'Genuinely moved, I stammered:

'"I can assure you, Monsieur Duché . . ."

'He went on:

'"You do know, I trust, that she was an innocent young lady?"

'Somehow, coming from him, the words didn't seem so comical. As it happens, it wasn't true. Annette was no longer an innocent young lady when I met her and she never made out that she was.

'The funny thing is, it was because of her father, indirectly, that she wasn't. He was a loner and there was only one person he admired, a man the same age as him, his superior at work. He held him in high regard – looked up to him, really; it was more a sort of hero-worship.

'Annette got a job as a typist in this man's office, and Duché felt the same pride in her as some fathers feel when their sons give their lives for their country.

'Stupid, eh? It was with this man that Annette had her first sexual experience, an incomplete one, as it happens, because of his impotence, but because she was obsessed with the memory of it, and to avoid a repeat performance, she came to Paris.

'I wasn't brave enough to raise this with her father. I kept quiet as I tried to find the right words.

'With a thick voice, he kept insisting:

'"Have you told your wife?"

'I told him I had, without thinking, without considering the consequences.

'"Has she agreed to the divorce?"

'I confess that I said yes to this too.'

Maigret, who was looking at him hard, asked his own question:

'Did you ever actually consider a divorce?'

'I don't know . . . You want the truth, don't you? Maybe the thought crossed my mind, but I never contemplated it seriously. I was happy . . . Well, let's just say that I had enough small pleasures in my life that I thought of myself as a happy man and I didn't feel brave enough to . . .'

He was still trying to find the exact words, but the exactness he was striving for was beyond his reach, so he rather gave up.

'In short, you had no reason to change the status quo?'

'It's more complicated than that. With Christine life had been . . . How shall I put it? . . . Life had been different. More colourful. Do you see what I'm saying? Then, little by little, reality began to intrude. I began to see her in a new light. I didn't hold it against her. I knew it was inevitable. I was the one who hadn't seen things as they were from the start.

'This other woman that Christine had become inspired my affection too, perhaps more so than the old Christine. But not rapture, not flights of passion. We were in new territory.'

He wiped his brow, an action that was starting to become repetitive.

'I really want you to believe me! I'm trying to help you understand everything. Annette is different from how Christine was. I'm different too. And I'm a lot older. I was happy with what she gave me and had no desire to know any more. Maybe you find that selfish, even cynical?'

'So you didn't want to make Annette your wife and repeat your first experience . . . Despite this, you told her father . . .'

'I don't remember the exact words I said. I felt ashamed with him sitting there in front of me. I felt guilty. Besides, I wanted to avoid a scene. I swore that I loved Annette, which is true. I promised to marry her as soon as I was able to.'

'Did you use those very words?'

'Maybe . . . In any case, I spoke passionately enough that Duché was moved . . . It would just be a case of sorting out the formalities, I said . . . To move on from this episode, I'll tell you just one detail that was even more absurd than the rest . . . Towards the end, I'd so much got into the role of the future son-in-law that I cracked open the bottle of champagne that we always kept in the fridge and we drank a toast . . .

'When I left the building it was already dark. I got into my car and drove around the streets at random.

'I didn't know if I had done the right thing or the wrong thing. I felt as if I had betrayed Christine . . . I have never been able to kill an animal. Once, however, I was visiting friends in the country, and they asked me to slit the throat of a chicken. I didn't want to lose face by refusing. Everybody was looking at me. It took me two attempts, and I felt as if I was carrying out an execution.

'In a way that was what I'd just done . . . Just because some half-drunk old man had played the offended father, I had denied fifteen years of life with Christine. I had promised, sworn, to sacrifice her.

'I too started drinking, in the first bar I came to. It wasn't far from Place de la République, as I found to my surprise a bit later. Then I went to the Champs-Élysées. Another bar. I downed three or four glasses one after the other, trying to work out what I was going to say to my wife.

'I composed sentences in my head and spoke them to myself in a soft voice, to check how they sounded.'

He looked at Maigret, pleadingly all of a sudden.

'I'm sorry. It's probably not the done thing . . . You wouldn't have something to drink, would you? I've held out up until now. But it's a physical thing, do you see? When you've had a lot to drink the night before . . .'

Maigret went to the cupboard, fetched the bottle of cognac and poured Josset a glass.

'Thank you. I still feel ashamed of myself. I've been like this since yesterday evening, since that grotesque scene, but it's not for the reasons people think.

'I didn't kill Christine. The idea didn't cross my mind for a moment. I tried to think up all sorts of solutions, I admit, some of them quite improbable ones, because now I was drunk too. But even if I had intended to kill her, I would have been physically incapable of doing it.'

The telephone still didn't ring at the Pardons'. So the little tailor wasn't dead yet, and his wife was still waiting while the children were no doubt asleep.

'At that point,' Maigret was saying, 'I thought that there was time . . .'

Time for what, he didn't specify.

'I was struggling to form an opinion, weighing up the pros and cons . . . My telephone rang. It was Janvier, asking me to come into the inspectors' room. I excused myself and went.

'Janvier wanted to show me the latest edition of one of the afternoon newspapers – the ink wasn't yet dry. A bold headline announced:

ADRIEN JOSSET'S DOUBLE LIFE

VIOLENT SCENE AT RUE CAULAINCOURT

'What about the other papers?'

'It's just this one.'

'Phone the newsroom and ask them where they got it from.'

While he waited, Maigret read the article:

We are able to provide some details on the private life of Adrien Josset, whose wife was murdered last night in their home in Auteuil (see article above).

While friends of the couple consider them to be close, in fact this manufacturer of pharmaceutical products has been leading a double life for about a year.

He has been having an affair with his secretary, Annette D—, 20, whom he has set up in an apartment in Rue Caulaincourt, where he picks her up every morning in his sports car and drops her off again almost every evening.

Two or three times a week, Adrien Josset had dinner with his mistress and he often spent the night there.

However, yesterday evening, a dramatic incident took place at Rue Caulaincourt. The young woman's father, a respectable civil servant from Fontenay-le-Comte, paid his daughter an unexpected visit and came across the couple in a situation of intimacy that left no room for doubt.

The two men confronted each other in a violent altercation. We have not been able to contact Monsieur D—, who must have left the capital this morning, but the events that played out in Rue Caulaincourt are evidently not unrelated to the drama that would unfold a short time later in the Josset home in Auteuil.

Janvier hung up.

'I couldn't get hold of the reporter, because he's not at the paper at present . . .'

'He's probably here, out in the corridor with the others.'

'Possibly. The person I spoke to was pretty tight-lipped. First of all, she mentioned an anonymous phone call to the newsroom around midnight, just after the crime had been announced on the radio. In the end I realized it must have been the concierge.'

Half an hour earlier, Josset had still had a chance to properly defend himself. He hadn't been charged. Even though he was considered a suspect, there was no material evidence against him.

Coméliau was sitting in his office, awaiting the result of the interrogation, and even though he was in a hurry to offer up the guilty party to the public, he would not have acted against Maigret's advice.

A concierge who wanted to get her photo in the papers had just changed the whole situation.

As far as the public were concerned, Josset would from now on be the man with the double life, and even the thousands of men in the same situation as him would not refrain from seeing that as the motive for the murder.

So true was this that Maigret could hear the phone in his office ringing already through the door. When he went in, Lapointe, who had picked up the phone, said:

'He's here, sir, I'll hand you over.'

Coméliau, obviously.

'Have you read it, Maigret?'

'I knew about it,' Maigret replied drily.

Josset couldn't fail to notice that it was about him and he cocked an ear.

'Was it you who gave the information to the paper? Did the concierge inform you?'

'No. *He* told me.'

'Of his own accord?'

'Yes.'

'So he really did meet the girl's father yesterday evening?'

'That's right.'

'Don't you think, under the circumstances—?'

'I don't know, sir. I'm still interrogating him.'

'Will you be much longer?'

'I don't think so.'

'Bring me up to date as soon as you can and don't tell the press anything until you've seen me.'

'I promise.'

Should he tell Josset about it? Would that be the honest thing to do? This phone call had clearly unnerved him.

'I guess the examining magistrate—'

'He won't do anything until he sees me. Sit down. Try to stay calm. I have a few more questions to ask you.'

'Something's happened, hasn't it?'

'Yes.'

'Something bad for me?'

'Fairly. I'll tell you about it in a moment. Where were you? . . . In a bar in the Étoile area . . . This will all be checked, not necessarily because we doubt your word, but because it's routine. Do you know the name of the bar?'

'The Select. Jean, the barman, has known me a long time.'

'What time was it?'

'I didn't look at my watch, or the clock behind the bar, but I'd say around nine thirty.'

'Did you speak to anyone?'

'The barman.'

'Did you mention your problems?'

'No. He realized, because of the way I was drinking. It's not my normal style. He said something like: "Everything OK, Monsieur Josset?"'

'I had to reply: "Not so good . . ."'

'Yes, that's it. Out of self-respect, so I wouldn't be taken for a drunk, I said: "I ate something that didn't agree with me."'

'So you were lucid, at least?'

'I knew where I was, what I was doing, where I had parked my car. A little while later, I stopped at a red light. Is that what you mean by lucid? It didn't mean that reality wasn't all out of kilter. The fact that I was feeling sorry for myself, so maudlin . . . I'm not normally like that.'

But he was a weak man, his story proved that abundantly, and it was no less visible in his face, his expressions.

'I kept saying to myself: "Why me?" I felt like I'd walked into a trap. I even suspected Annette of tipping off her father and getting him to come to Paris to provoke a scene and back me into a corner.

'At other times, I blamed Christine. They will all make out that I owe my success, and the fact I have become an important person, to her . . . Maybe that's true. Who knows what my career would have been without her?

'But she also dragged me into a world that wasn't mine, where I have never felt at home. It's only at work that I . . .'

He shook his head.

'When I'm less tired I'll try to be more coherent . . . Christine taught me a lot. There was both good and bad in her. She isn't a happy person and never has been . . . I was about to add that she never will be . . . You can see I still can't believe that she is dead. Doesn't it prove that I didn't do it?'

It didn't prove a thing, as Maigret had learned from long experience.

'When you left the Select, did you head home?'

'Yes.'

'To do what?'

'To talk to Christine, tell her everything, discuss with her what we should do next.'

'At that moment, did you consider the possibility of a divorce?'

'It seemed the most obvious solution, but . . .'

'But?'

'I realized it would be difficult to get my wife to accept the idea. You'd need to know her to understand. Even her friends know only superficial things about her. Our relationship was not on the same footing as it was before, that's true. We were no longer in love, as I've told you. We had started to argue and perhaps even despise each other. But I was the only person who understood her, she knew it. She could only be herself with me. I didn't judge her. Wouldn't she have missed me? She was so afraid of ending up alone! It's because of this that she hated growing old so much, because in her mind old age and solitude were synonymous.

'"As long as I have money I can pay for company, can't I?" She would say that as a joke, but it represented what she really thought.

'Was I just going to come out with it and tell her I was leaving her?'

'But you made your mind up that you would?'

'Yes . . . Not exactly . . . Not just like that . . . I would have described the scene in Rue Caulaincourt and I would have asked her advice.'

'Did you often ask her advice?'

'Yes.'

'Even about business?'

'On important business matters, yes.'

'Do you think it was purely out of honesty that you felt the need to tell her about your relationship with Annette?'

He thought about this, genuinely surprised by the question.

'I see what you mean . . . First of all, there was an age difference between us. When I met her, I was very unfamiliar with Paris and had only seen the bits that are accessible to a penniless student. She taught me every-thing about a whole way of life, a whole social milieu . . .'

'What happened when you got to Rue Lopert?'

'I wondered if Christine would be home. It was unlikely, and I anticipated having to wait for a while. I was com-forted by the thought, as I needed to screw up my courage.'

'By having another drink?'

'I guess so. Once you start, it's easy to believe that one more drink will steady your nerves. I saw the Cadillac parked at the door.'

'And were the lights on inside the house?'

'I saw just one – in Carlotta's room on the top floor. I used my key to go in.'

'Did you bolt the door after you?'

'I was expecting that question, since they asked me the same thing this morning. I suppose I must have done it automatically, because I usually do, but I simply can't recall.'

'Were you still unaware of the time?'

'No. I looked at the clock in the hall. It was five past ten.'

'Were you surprised that your wife was home so soon?'

'No. She doesn't live by fixed rules, so it is difficult to know what she might do at any given time.'

He continued to talk about her in the present tense, as if she were still alive.

'Have you been to our house?' he asked Maigret in turn.

Maigret had just given it a cursory viewing, as the pub-lic prosecutor's men were at the scene, as well as Doctor Paul, the local chief inspector and seven or eight experts from Criminal Records.

'I'll have to go back,' he muttered.

'You'll find a bar on the ground floor.'

The ground floor was in fact a single room, broken up by various partitions and unexpected recesses, which Maigret remembered was as big as the bars you find along the Champs-Élysées.

'I poured myself a glass of whisky. It's all my wife will drink. I sank into an armchair. I needed a bit of breathing space.'

'Did you turn on the lights?'

'In the hall, when I came in, but I turned them off again straight away. There are no shutters on the windows. There is a streetlamp just ten metres from the house, which casts enough light to see in the room. Besides, it was an almost full moon. I seem to remember spending some time looking at it and I even imagined it witnessing my misfortune . . .

'I got up to pour myself another drink. We have very large glasses. Then I returned to my chair, whisky in hand, and carried on pondering.

'And that, inspector, is how I came to fall asleep.

'The inspector this morning didn't believe me. He advised me to change my line of defence, and when I refused he got angry.

'But it's the truth. If it all took place while I was asleep, I wouldn't have heard a thing. I didn't dream either. I can't remember anything, except a black hole – I can't think of another word for it.

'I gradually woke up with a pain in my side, a sort of cramp.

'I took a while to gather my wits before getting up.'

'Did you feel drunk?'

'I couldn't honestly say. It all seems a nightmare to me now. I switched on the light, drank a glass of water, unsure about drinking any more spirits. Then I went upstairs.'

'With the intention of waking your wife and discussing your situation with her?'

He didn't reply but simply looked at Maigret in astonishment, almost a look of reproach. He seemed to be saying: 'You are asking me that?'

It made Maigret feel a little embarrassed, and he murmured:

'Go on.'

'I went into my room, where I turned on the light and looked at myself in the mirror. I had a headache. My unshaven face and the bags under my eyes disgusted me.

'Mechanically I opened Christine's door . . . That's when I saw her as you saw her there this morning.'

The body half out of the bed, the head dangling over a fur rug splashed with blood, as were the sheets and the satin coverlet on the bed.

On a cursory examination, Doctor Paul – who was currently conducting a full post-mortem – counted twenty-three wounds inflicted by what the report called, in standard terminology, a sharp instrument.

So sharp, in fact, and wielded with such ferocity that the head was almost completely severed.

Silence reigned in Maigret's office. It seemed inconceivable that outside the windows life went on at its usual pace, that the sun was shining and the air felt so warm.

Tramps were sleeping under Pont Saint-Michel with newspapers over their faces, oblivious to the noise. And two lovers sat on the stone wall, swinging their legs over the water, which showed their reflection.

'Try to remember every last detail.'

Josset nodded.

'Did you turn the light on in your wife's room?'

'I wasn't brave enough.'

'Did you go up to her?'

'I kept my distance.'

'You didn't check that she was dead?'

'It was obvious.'

'What was your first reaction?'

'To make a call . . . I went to the telephone and even picked it up . . .'

'To call whom?'

'I didn't know. I didn't think about the police straight away. I thought of our doctor first, Doctor Badel, who is a friend.'

'Why did you not alert him?'

Without missing a beat, he replied:

'I don't know.'

He put his head in his hands – either he was pensive or he was a good actor.

'It was the words, I think, that stopped me phoning . . . What would I say? "Someone has killed Christine. Come . . ."?

'Then they would ask me questions. The police would come into my house. I was in no state to face that. I feared that I would fall apart at the smallest push . . .'

'You weren't alone in the house. The maid was sleeping upstairs.'

'Yes. Everything I did seems illogical, yet there must be some logic to it because I did what I did and I am not mad.

'There is also the fact that I had to dash into the bathroom to throw up . . . That created a sort of interval. As I leaned over the sink I started to think. I told myself that no one would believe me, that I would be arrested and questioned and locked up . . .

'And I felt so tired! If only I could have a few hours, a few days . . . Not to run away, but to be able to take a step back. Maybe it's what people call panic? Has no one ever said that to you?'

What Josset didn't know was that many others had passed through this same office before him just as exhausted, just as haggard-looking, and had slowly spun their tissue of lies or of unspeakable truths.

'I washed my face with cold water and looked at myself in the mirror again. Then I rubbed my hands over my cheeks and started to shave.'

'Why, *exactly*, did you have a shave?'

'I was thinking quickly, and probably not thinking straight, trying to sort out the jumble of thoughts in my head.

'I decided to go away. Not by car, because there was a risk of being spotted too soon, and besides I didn't feel strong enough to drive for hours. The simplest way was to catch a plane at Orly, any plane. I often have to travel on business, sometimes at short notice, and my passport always has a number of current visas.

'I worked out how long it would take me to get to Orly. I had very little money on me, maybe twenty or thirty thousand francs, and there was unlikely to be much more in my wife's room, as we had got into the habit of paying for everything by cheque. That was a complication.

'These various preoccupations stopped me thinking about what had happened to Christine. My mind focused on the small details. It was one such detail that led me to have a shave. The customs officers at Orly know me, and know that I am very careful, almost fastidious, about my appearance. They would have been surprised to see me turn up unshaven.

'I had to pass by the office in Avenue Marceau. There wasn't exactly a fortune in the safe there, but I knew I would at least find a few hundred thousand.

'I needed a suitcase too, if only for appearances' sake, and I packed one with a suit, some underwear, a toilet bag . . . I thought about taking my watches. I have four altogether, and two of them are quite valuable. I'd be able to sell them if I needed some cash.

'The watches reminded me of my wife's jewellery . . . I just had no idea what lay ahead. I might take a flight to the far end of Europe or South America . . . I wasn't even sure if I'd take Annette or not.'

'Did you consider taking her?'

'I believe I did, yes. So as not to be on my own, partly. Out of a sense of duty too.'

'Not for love?'

'I don't think so. I'm being honest. Our love was . . .'

He corrected himself:

'Our love *is* something that exists in a particular con-
text: the office that we share, the daily car journey from
Rue Caulaincourt to Avenue Marceau, our dinners in her
little apartment . . . I just couldn't see Annette with me in
Brussels, London or Buenos Aires, for example.'

'Nevertheless, you planned to take her with you?'

'Maybe because of the promise I made her father . . .
Then I was afraid that he might have stayed the night at
Rue Caulaincourt. What would I say to him if I came face
to face with him in the middle of the night?'

'Did you take your wife's jewels?'

'Some of them, the ones she kept in her dressing table,
in other words, the ones she had been wearing recently.'

'Did you do anything else?'

He hesitated, lowered his head.

'No. I can't think of anything. I turned out the lights. I
went downstairs without making a sound . . . I even
thought about having another drink, since my stomach
was churning, but I resisted.'

'Did you take your car?'

'I decided that wouldn't be wise. Carlotta might have
heard the engine and come downstairs. Who knows? There
is a taxi stand at the Auteuil church, so I walked there.'

He grabbed his empty glass and handed it to Maigret
with a timid expression.

'May I?'

4. What Adrien Josset Did Next That Night

One time, when comparing the Paris police's famously tough grillings with the equally well-known American 'third degree', Maigret had suggested that the suspects most likely to get away with it are the idiots. This nugget was subsequently picked up by a journalist, with the result that it was periodically trotted out in the press, with minor variations.

What he had been trying to say, in fact, was something that he still believed to be true: that a simple-minded man is naturally mistrustful, always on the defensive; he uses the minimum number of words to answer questions, makes no attempt at plausibility and later, when confronted with his self-contradictions, is not knocked off his stride but sticks firmly to his statement.

On the other hand, the intelligent man feels the need to explain himself, to clear up all doubts in the mind of his interrogator. In an effort to sound convincing, he anticipates questions, provides an excess of detail and, by trying hard to construct a watertight story, ends up getting caught out.

And once his contradictions are exposed, he nearly always becomes flustered and, ashamed of himself, decides to own up.

Adrien Josset was one of those who anticipated the questions, anxious to explain facts and actions that at first sight seemed incoherent.

He didn't just concede this incoherence, he made a point of emphasizing it; he talked about it out loud as if he were trying to uncover the underlying logic.

Guilty or innocent, he was familiar enough with the workings of an investigation to know that, once it had swung into action, sooner or later everything he had done that night would be fed through the mechanism.

He was so keen to say everything that on two or three occasions Maigret had almost called a halt to this sort of confessional flow that, to his mind, was premature.

Maigret usually decided on the moment of truth himself. He preferred to wait until he had a more complete and more personal understanding of a case. That morning he had barely even had a look at the house in Rue Lopert and he knew nothing of its inhabitants and next to nothing about the crime itself.

He hadn't questioned anyone: neither the Spanish maid nor Madame Siran, the cook, whose son worked for the Métro and who went home to Javel every evening.

He knew nothing about the neighbours, had never seen Annette Duché or her father, who had come running from Fontenay-le-Comte in response to some mysterious summons. He still hadn't seen the offices of the pharmaceutical company Josset et Virieu on Avenue Marceau and hadn't met any of Josset's friends or any number of other people of varying importance.

Doctor Paul had finished his post-mortem and must have been surprised not to have received the usual telephone call from the inspector, who was rarely patient enough to wait for his written report. Upstairs in

Criminal Records too they were examining the evidence found that morning.

Torrence, Lucas and perhaps ten other officers would according to routine be questioning Carlotta and other minor witnesses in various offices around police headquarters.

Maigret could easily have interrupted the interrogation to find out what was going on; Lapointe, for one, sitting hunched over his notepad, was surprised to see him listening so patiently, not trying to steer the conversation, not trying to catch Josset out.

The questions he asked were rarely technical ones, and some seemed to have only a distant relevance to the events of the previous night.

'Tell me, Monsieur Josset, at your offices in Avenue Marceau or your laboratory at Saint-Mandé you must sometimes have had occasion to sack one of your employees?'

'That happens in any business.'

'Do you deal with it personally?'

'No. I leave all that to Monsieur Jules.'

'Have you ever had any problems of a business nature?'

'That's inevitable too. Three years ago, for example, someone questioned the purity of one of our products and claimed it had had harmful effects.'

'Who dealt with that?'

'Monsieur Jules.'

'The way I understood it, he is the head of personnel rather than a commercial director. It seems that—'

Maigret broke off, then after a moment or two's thought, went on:

'You don't like having to tell people bad news, do you? I note that when you were with Monsieur Duché in Rue Caulaincourt you promised him anything – to divorce your wife, to marry Annette – rather than be up-front with him.

'When you found your wife dead, you avoided going up to her and you didn't even turn on the light. Your first thought was to leave . . .'

Josset hung his head.

'It's true. I panicked. There's no other way of putting it.'

'Did you get a taxi from the Auteuil church?'

'Yes. A grey 403. The driver had a southern accent.'

'Did you take the taxi to Avenue Marceau?'

'Yes.'

'What time was it?'

'I don't know.'

'You must have driven past several lit-up clocks. You were intending to catch a plane. You often travel by plane. So you must know the timetables of a certain number of airlines. Knowing the right time is an important thing for you.'

'I accept all that, but I can't come up with any explanation. Things don't happen the way you expect them to when you think about them with a clear head.'

'Did you have the taxi wait for you at Avenue Marceau?'

'I didn't want to attract attention. I paid the fare and walked across the pavement. For a moment, as I searched through my pockets, I thought I had forgotten my key.'

'Were you worried?'

'No. I intended to leave, but I was in the hands of fate. Anyway, I eventually found the key in a pocket I don't usually put it in. I entered the building.'

'Wasn't there a risk you would wake up the concierge?'

'If I had, I would have said that I needed certain documents for a business trip that had been arranged at the last minute. I wasn't too concerned about that.'

'Did he hear you?'

'No. I went up to my office. I opened the safe, took the 400,000 francs that were inside and then wondered where to conceal them, in case I got searched by customs. But I didn't attach too much importance to that, as they never searched me . . . I sat in my normal chair and stayed there motionless for ten minutes, looking all around me.'

'Is that when you made your mind up not to leave?'

'I felt too tired. I didn't have the strength . . .'

'The strength to do what?'

'To go to Orly, to buy a ticket, to wait, to show my passport, to feel afraid . . .'

'Afraid of being arrested?'

'Of being questioned. I kept thinking about Carlotta, who had perhaps come downstairs. Even when I landed in a foreign airport there was the risk I might be questioned. At best, I'd be starting a new life, with nobody . . .'

'Did you put the money back in the safe?'

'Yes.'

'What did you do next?'

'I felt encumbered by the suitcase. I wanted a drink. It was an obsession. I was convinced that a bit of alcohol would restore my composure, even though it hadn't worked that well so far. I must have walked as far as Étoile to hail another taxi. I said:

'"Stop when you see a bar."

'The car only had to go 200 metres. I left the suitcase and went inside, without realizing it was a strip joint. I told the maître d' I didn't want a table and went to the bar instead, where I ordered a whisky. A hostess asked me to buy her a drink, and for the sake of peace I nodded to the barman to serve her.

'I had two drinks. I paid. I left and went to find my taxi.

'"Which station?" the driver asked.

'"Go to Auteuil. Go via Rue Chardon-Lagache. I'll tell you where to stop."

'My suitcase was giving me a guilt complex. I stopped the taxi 150 metres from my house and made sure before I went in that there were no lights on in the house. I didn't hear a sound. I turned on only the lamps I needed and I returned my wife's jewels as well as my clothes and bathroom things to their proper places. I guess you will find my fingerprints on the dressing table and the jewellery, if you haven't already.'

'So you went back into your wife's room?'

'I had to.'

'You didn't look at her?'

'No.'

'You still didn't think of ringing the police?'

'I was still putting it off.'

'What did you do next?'

'I went out and walked round the streets.'

'In which direction?'

Josset hesitated, and Maigret, who was watching him, frowned and then said impatiently:

'It's a neighbourhood with which you are familiar, in which you have lived for fifteen years. Even if you were preoccupied, or in a daze, you must have recognized some of the places you passed.'

'I can clearly remember being at Pont Mirabeau, without any recollection of how I got there.'

'Did you cross the bridge?'

'Not all the way. I leaned on the parapet near the middle and watched the Seine flow by.'

'What was on your mind?'

'The fact that I would probably be arrested and for weeks, if not months, I would have a whole lot of painful and exhausting problems to deal with.'

'Did you retrace your steps?'

'Yes. I would have loved to have another drink before going to the police station, but there were no bars open in the neighbourhood. I almost took a taxi – again.'

'Does Annette Duché have a telephone?'

'I had her get one put in.'

'And at no point did you think of ringing her to tell her what was going on?'

He pondered for a moment.

'Maybe. I don't know now. In any case, I didn't do it.'

'Did you ever at any point wonder who might have killed your wife?'

'Mostly, I was thinking that I would be the one accused of it.'

'According to the report I have here before me, you turned up at the police station in Auteuil, at the corner of Boulevard Exelmans and Rue Chardon-Lagache, at three thirty. You gave your identity card to the desk sergeant and asked to speak to the chief inspector in person. You were told that it wasn't possible at that hour and you were taken instead to the office of Inspector Jeannet.'

'He didn't say what his name was.'

'The inspector questioned you briefly and then, after you had handed over your key, sent a car round to Rue Lopert . . . I have here the more detailed statements you made later. I haven't read them yet. Are they accurate?'

'I suppose they are. It was very hot in the office. It made me feel very sluggish, and I could have happily fallen asleep. And I found the inspector's aggressive and sarcastic tone very off-putting.'

'It appears that you did in fact fall asleep for two hours.'

'I didn't know how long it was.'

'Do you have anything you wish to add?'

'I don't think so. Maybe later something will come back to me. I feel exhausted. I feel like everything is stacked against me, that the truth will never come out . . . I didn't kill Christine. I have never in my life set out to hurt anyone . . . Do you believe me?'

'I don't have an opinion . . . Will you go and type all this up, Lapointe?'

Then, to Josset:

'You've had enough for now. When they bring you the typed document, I want you to read it and sign it.'

He went out into the adjoining office and sent Janvier in to sit with Josset in his place. The interrogation had lasted three hours.

★

Maigret paused and let his gaze linger on the lights along Boulevard Voltaire. He heard his wife give a small cough. He turned towards her, and she gave him a subtle signal.

She was reminding him of the time. They had stayed much later than usual. Alice was saying goodbye to her mother as she and her husband had to get back to Maisons-Alfort, where they lived. Pardon kissed his daughter on her forehead.

'Goodnight!'

Just as the young couple were going out of the door, the telephone rang; somehow it sounded more strident than usual. Madame Pardon looked at her husband, who walked slowly over to answer it.

'Doctor Pardon speaking . . .'

It was Madame Kruger, whose voice was not as shrill and resonating as before. Now it was a barely audible murmur to those not right next to the telephone.

'No, no,' Pardon was telling her gently. 'You mustn't blame yourself. It's not your fault, I assure you . . . Are the children up? Is there a neighbour who could look after them? . . . Listen, I'll be there in half an hour at the latest.'

He listened for a while longer, saying a few words now and then.

'Yes . . . Yes . . . You did everything you could . . . I'll take care of it . . . Yes . . . Yes . . . I'll be there soon . . .'

He hung up and gave a sigh. Maigret stood up. Madame Maigret had folded up her knitting and pulled on her raincoat.

'Is he dead?'

'A few minutes ago . . . I have to go over there right now. She will need my help.'

They walked down the stairs together. The doctor's car was parked by the pavement.

'Would you like me to drop you off?'

'No thanks, we'd rather walk for a bit.'

That was part of the tradition. Madame Maigret automatically took her husband's arm, and they made their way along the deserted road in the peace and quiet of the evening.

'Was it the Josset case you were talking about?'

'Yes.'

'Did you get to the end?'

'No. I'll pick it up again another time.'

'You did everything that you could . . .'

'Like Pardon this evening . . . Like the tailor's wife.'

She gripped his arm more tightly.

'It's not your fault.'

'I know.'

There were a few cases he didn't like to remember, and, paradoxically, they were the ones he had taken most to heart.

To Pardon, the Jewish tailor in Rue Popincourt had originally been a stranger, just one sick person among many. Now, because of a shrill voice on the telephone, a decision made at the end of a family dinner, a few words spoken out of weariness, Maigret was sure his friend would never forget him.

Josset too had been much in Maigret's thoughts for a long time.

While Lapointe was typing up his notes, telephones were ringing all around the offices, and the journalists and photographers waited impatiently in the corridor, Maigret wandered round police headquarters, with a serious and preoccupied air, his shoulders hunched.

As he had expected, he found the Spanish maid in one of the offices at the back, being questioned by big Torrence. She was around thirty, fairly pretty, with a cheeky expression but thin, hard lips.

Maigret looked her up and down for a moment, then turned to Torrence.

'What did she say?'

'She doesn't know anything. She was asleep and was woken by the Auteuil police, who were making a racket downstairs.'

'What time did her mistress get home?'

'She doesn't know.'

'She wasn't in the house at the time?'

'I'd been allowed to go out,' the young woman chipped in.

No one had asked her, but her nose was out of joint at how little attention they were paying her.

'She was meeting someone by the river,' Torrence explained.

'At what time?'

'Eight thirty.'

'When did she get back?'

'Eleven.'

'Did she see any lights on in the house?'

'She claims she didn't.'

'I'm not claiming anything. I didn't.'

She still had a strong accent.

'Did you come in through the large room on the ground floor?' Maigret asked her.

'No. I came in through the service entrance.'

'Were there any cars parked in front of the house?'

'Madame's was the only one I saw.'

'What about Monsieur's?'

'I didn't notice.'

'When you come home, don't you normally check to see if you're needed for anything?'

'No. What they do in the evening has nothing to do with me.'

'Did you hear any sounds?'

'I'd have said if I had.'

'Did you go to sleep straight away?'

'As soon as I had had a wash.'

Maigret growled to Torrence:

'Find her boyfriend and check.'

Carlotta's resentful gaze followed him to the door.

In the inspectors' room he picked up one of the phones.

'Could you put me on to Doctor Paul, please? He may still be at the Forensic Institute. If not, ring his home number.'

He had to wait a few minutes.

'Maigret here. Any news?'

He automatically jotted down some notes, which was unnecessary, as he would be receiving the full report a short while later.

The wound to the throat was the first one inflicted and had been sufficient to cause death within a minute at most. The killer had then continued to stab the body in a frenzy, even though it was drained of blood . . .

The alcohol levels in the blood indicated, according to the medical examiner, that Christine Josset was drunk at the moment she was attacked.

She hadn't had any dinner. Her stomach contained no undigested food.

Finally, her liver was in a rather bad state.

As for the time of death, Doctor Paul could only say it was between ten in the evening and one in the morning.

'Can't you be more precise?'

'Not right now. One last detail might be of interest to you, however. The woman had had sex a few hours before she died.'

'Could it have been as little as half an hour?'

'It's not out of the question.'

'Ten minutes?'

'I can't give a scientific answer to that.'

'Thank you, doctor.'

'What is he saying?'

'Who?'

'The husband.'

'That he's innocent.'

'Do you believe him?'

'I don't know.'

Another telephone rang. An inspector waved to Maigret to indicate it was for him.

'Is that you, Maigret? Coméliau here. Is the interrogation over?'

'A few moments ago.'

'I'd like to see you.'

'I'm on my way.'

He was about to go out when Bonfils came in, looking excited.

'I was just about to knock on your door, chief. I've just got back from there. I spent two hours with Madame Siran, questioning her and making a closer inspection of the house. I have some news.'

'What is it?'

'Has Josset confessed?'

'No.'

'Did he say anything about a dagger?'

'What dagger?'

'We were busy searching Josset's room, Madame Siran and I, when I saw her looking for something. She seemed puzzled. It was hard to get her to talk, because I think she prefers her master to her mistress – she doesn't seem to have a very high opinion of her. In the end, she murmured: "The German dagger."'

'It's one of those commando knives which some people keep as a souvenir of the war.'

Maigret looked surprised.

'Josset was a commando in the war?'

'No. He wasn't in the war. He had an exemption. It was someone in his office, a certain Monsieur Jules, who brought it back and gave it to him.'

'What did Josset do with it?'

'Nothing. It was left on top of a small desk, in the bedroom, and was probably used as a paper knife . . . Anyway, it's disappeared.'

'How long ago?'

'It's been gone since this morning. Madame Siran is sure about that. She's the one who looks after her master's bedroom while the Spanish girl takes care of Madame Josset's room and her things.'

'Did you look everywhere?'

'I searched the house from top to bottom, including the cellar and the attic.'

Maigret was about to go back to his office to ask Josset about it. He didn't do so, because he had the examining magistrate waiting for him, and Coméliau was not very accommodating; besides, he needed time to think.

He walked through the glass door separating the Police Judiciaire from the Palais de Justice, weaved his way down a number of corridors and knocked on the door of an office he knew very well.

'Take a seat, Maigret.'

The afternoon papers were spread out on the desk, with their banner headlines and photos.

'Have you read these?'

'Yes.'

'Is he still denying it?'

'Yes.'

'But he admits that the scene in Rue Caulaincourt took place yesterday evening, a few hours before his wife was killed?'

'He told me about it of his own accord.'

'I assume he is claiming it is a coincidence?'

As usual, Coméliau was getting wound up, and his moustache was twitching.

'At eight o'clock in the evening, a father was with his twenty-year-old daughter, whom Josset had taken as his mistress. The two men confronted each other, and the father demanded redress.'

Maigret sighed wearily.

'Josset promised him he'd get a divorce.'

'And marry the girl?'

'Yes.'

'To do that he'd have to give up his fortune and his career.'

'That's not entirely true. For the last few years Josset has been a third owner of the pharmaceutical firm.'

'Do you think his wife would have agreed to a divorce?'

'I don't think anything, sir.'

'Where is he now?'

'In my office. One of my inspectors is typing up the transcript of the interrogation. Josset will read it and sign it.'

'And then? What do you plan to do with him?'

Coméliau could sense Maigret's reticence, and it made him angry.

'I suppose that now you're going to ask me to set him free and suggest I have him put under surveillance by one of your officers in the hope that he will give himself away somehow or other.'

'No.'

That wrong-footed the examining magistrate.

'Do you think he's guilty?'

'I don't know.'

'Listen, Maigret, if there's ever been an open-and-shut

case, it's this one. Four or five friends of mine, who know Josset and his wife well, have phoned me . . .'

'They spoke against him?'

'They have always seen him for what he is.'

'Which is what?'

'An ambitious, unscrupulous character who took advantage of Christine's passionate feelings for him. Only, once she started to grow old and lose her looks, he felt the need for a younger mistress and didn't hesitate . . .'

'I'll send you the transcript once it is finished.'

'And until then?'

'I'll keep Josset in my office. You can decide.'

'It wouldn't go down well if I released him, Maigret.'

'I can see that.'

'No one, do you hear, no one will believe he is innocent. I'm willing to read your document before I sign the committal, but you can safely assume that my mind is now made up.'

He didn't like the look on Maigret's face and he called him back.

'Do you have any argument to offer in his favour?'

Maigret didn't respond. He didn't have an argument. Only that Josset had told him that he didn't kill his wife.

And maybe that the whole thing seemed too simple, too obvious?

He returned to his office, where Janvier pointed out that the man had fallen asleep in his chair.

'You can go. Tell Lapointe that I'm back.'

Maigret sat down in his chair, fiddled with his pipes,

chose one and lit it. Josset opened his eyes and looked at him silently.

'Would you like to carry on sleeping?'

'No. I'm so sorry. Have you been here long?'

'Just a few moments.'

'Did you see the examining magistrate?'

'I've just come from there.'

'Am I being arrested?'

'I believe so.'

'It was bound to happen, wasn't it?'

'Do you know a good lawyer?'

'I count several of them as friends, but I wonder if I wouldn't prefer having a complete stranger.'

'Tell me something, Josset . . .'

The man shuddered, realizing that those simple words were the prelude to something unpleasant.

'Yes?'

'Where did you hide the knife?'

There was a brief hesitation.

'I was wrong. I should have told you about that . . .'

'You threw it into the Seine from Pont Mirabeau, is that correct?'

'Has it been found?'

'Not yet. Tomorrow the divers will go down and will find it.'

The man said nothing.

'Did you kill Christine?'

'No.'

'Nevertheless, you went to the effort of going all the way to Pont Mirabeau to throw your knife into the river.'

'No one will believe me, not even you.'

That 'not even you' was meant as a compliment to Maigret.

'Tell me the truth.'

'It was when I returned to put my suitcase away. In my room I spotted the dagger . . .'

'Did it have bloodstains on it?'

'No. At that point, I thought about what I would tell the police. I realized already that my story lacked credibility. I had tried not to look at the body, but the little I had seen suggested that the weapon involved had been a knife.

'When I saw mine lying there in full view on my desk I told myself the police would not fail to make a connection . . .'

'Because there was no blood on it!'

'If I had killed her and there had been some, wouldn't I have gone to the effort to clean the blade? I only thought about it when I had finished packing my case and was contemplating catching a plane. The knife lying there just a short distance from the body seemed damning, so I took it with me . . . It was Carlotta who told you, wasn't it? She's never been able to stand me.'

'It was Madame Siran.'

'That surprises me somewhat. But I should have expected it. From now on I don't suppose I can rely on anyone.'

Lapointe came into the office, holding the typed pages, which he put down in front of Maigret. Maigret handed one copy to Josset and started to peruse the second.

'Order a diver for tomorrow morning. Dawn at Pont Mirabeau.'

One hour later, the photographers finally got to take their pictures of Adrien Josset as he left Maigret's office with handcuffs on his wrists.

It was precisely because of the reporters and the photographers that Examining Magistrate Coméliau had insisted on the handcuffs.

5. Doctor Liorant's Obstinate Silence

Certain details of the case were etched more sharply than others in Maigret's memory. Even years later he could recall the particular taste and smell of the rain shower in Rue Caulaincourt as keenly as a childhood memory.

It was six thirty in the evening, and when the rain started it did not obscure the sun, already red above the rooftops. The sky remained ablaze, the windows shimmering with reflected light, and only a single pearl-grey cloud, slightly darker at the centre and glowing at its edges, floated over the streets, as light as a balloon.

There hadn't been any rain anywhere else in Paris. Madame Maigret confirmed that evening that none had fallen in Boulevard Richard-Lenoir.

The raindrops were more transparent, as if more liquid, than usual, and when the shower began they made big black circles in the dust of the pavement as they landed one by one.

Raising his head, Maigret saw four pots of geraniums on a window-sill and got hit on his eyelid by a raindrop that was so large it almost hurt.

He assumed that the open window meant that Annette was home and he went inside the building, past the lodge, and looked in vain for a lift. He was about to go up the stairs when a door opened behind him and a not too friendly voice called out:

'Where are you going?'

He found himself face to face with the concierge, who looked nothing like the person he had imagined from listening to Josset's account. He had expected her to be of a certain age, rather slovenly. In fact, she was a pleasant and attractive woman of about thirty. Only her vulgar, aggressive voice set a false note.

'To Mademoiselle Duché's,' he replied politely.

'She's not home.'

Later, looking back on this moment, he would wonder why it is that certain people are unpleasant from the start, for no obvious reason.

'She's due home soon, isn't she?'

'She comes and goes when she pleases.'

'Were you the one who rang the paper?'

She stood on the threshold of the glass door but didn't invite him in.

'What about it?' she replied defiantly.

'I'm from the police.'

'I know. I recognized you. You don't impress me.'

'When Monsieur Duché came here to see his daughter, did he tell you his name?'

'He even stayed in the lodge for quarter of an hour and had a chat.'

'So he had come once before, when his daughter wasn't here? During the afternoon, presumably?'

'Around five o'clock.'

'Was it you who wrote to him in Fontenay?'

'If I had, I would have been simply fulfilling my duty, and it would be of no concern to anyone. But it wasn't me. It was the young lady's aunt.'

'Do you know her aunt?'

'We go to the same shops.'

'Did you inform her about what was going on?'

'She had her own suspicions already.'

'Did she tell you she was going to write?'

'We talked about it.'

'When Monsieur Duché arrived, did you talk to him about Monsieur Josset?'

'I answered his questions and advised him to come back later, after seven.'

'Did you tell the young lady about this when she got home?'

'I'm not paid to do that.'

'Was Monsieur Duché very angry?'

'He was struggling to believe it, the poor man.'

'Did you go up after him to find out what was happening?'

'I took a letter up to the fifth floor.'

'Did you stop on the landing on the fourth floor?'

'Maybe I paused for breath for a short while. What do you want me to say?'

'You mentioned a violent altercation.'

'To whom?'

'To the reporter.'

'The papers print whatever they like. Look! Here she is, *your* young lady!'

It wasn't one young lady but two who came into the

building and headed towards the stairs without a glance at the concierge and Maigret. The first one was blonde and looked very young. She was wearing a navy-blue suit and a light-coloured hat. The second was thinner, harder-looking; she was about thirty-five and walked like a man.

'I thought you came to speak to her.'

Maigret suppressed his anger, because her gratuitous unpleasantness was really getting to him.

'I will speak to her, never fear. I may well need to speak to you again.'

He felt bad about this implied threat, which had a hint of childishness about it. He waited to go upstairs until he heard a door open and close up above.

On the third floor he paused a moment to get his breath back, then carried on up and knocked on the door. He could hear whispers, then footsteps. It wasn't Annette who opened the door a crack, but her companion.

'What is it?'

'Detective Chief Inspector Maigret, Police Judiciaire.'

'Annette, it's the police!'

Annette must have been in the bedroom, perhaps changing out of her wet clothes.

'I'm coming.'

It was all a bit of a let-down. The geraniums were there all right, but they were the only detail that corresponded to the mental image Maigret had formed of the place. The apartment was very ordinary-looking, lacking in any personal touches. The famous kitchen-diner, where their little dinners took place, had dull grey walls and the sort of furniture you find in low-budget rented rooms.

Annette wasn't changing, she was just combing her hair. She too was a bit of a disappointment. True, she was smooth-skinned, in the way that twenty-year-olds are, but rather ordinary, with large, somewhat protuberant blue eyes. She reminded Maigret of the portraits you saw in the windows of provincial photographers', and he would bet any money that by the time she was forty she would be a large woman with her lips set in a hard line.

'Excuse me, mademoiselle . . .'

Her friend headed for the door, somewhat reluctantly.

'I'll be off . . .'

'Why? You're not in the way.'

And to Maigret:

'This is Jeanine, who also works at Avenue Marceau. She was kind enough to walk me home. Please take a seat, inspector.'

He couldn't quite put a finger on what didn't feel right. He was slightly annoyed that Josset had given this young woman such a build-up; although her eyes were a little red, she hardly seemed devastated.

'Has he been arrested?' she asked as she tidied up around her.

'The examining magistrate signed a custodial order this afternoon.'

'How did he take it?'

Jeanine advised her:

'It might be best if you let the inspector speak.'

This wasn't a formal interrogation, and Coméliau would no doubt be furious to learn that Maigret had taken it upon himself to come here.

'What time was it when you heard what had happened?'

'Just as we were about to leave the office for lunch. One of the warehousemen had a transistor radio. He was talking to some others about the news, and Jeanine passed it on to me.'

'Did you go out for lunch as usual?'

'What could I do?'

'She wasn't hungry, inspector. I had to cheer her up. She was crying the whole time.'

'Is your father still in Paris?'

'He left this morning at nine o'clock. He wanted to return to Fontenay today, as he has taken only two days off work and has to be back at the préfecture tomorrow.'

'Did he stay in a hotel?'

'Yes. Near the station. I don't know which one.'

'Did he stay here long yesterday evening?'

'About an hour or so. He was tired.'

'Did Josset promise him that he would get a divorce and marry you?'

She reddened and looked across at her companion, as if seeking advice.

'Did Adrien tell you that?'

'Did he?'

'The matter was discussed.'

'Was it a formal promise?'

'I believe so.'

'Before that, did you have hopes he might marry you one day?'

'I didn't think about it.'

'He didn't speak to you about the future?'

'No . . . only in a vague way.'

'Were you happy?'

'He was very nice to me, very attentive.'

Maigret didn't hazard to ask if she loved him, because he feared she would lie again, and Annette asked him:

'Do you think he will be found guilty?'

'Do you think that he killed his wife?'

She blushed and looked to her companion again for support.

'I don't know . . . It's what they're saying on the radio, and in the papers . . .'

'You know him well. Do you think he is capable of killing his wife?'

Instead of replying directly, she murmured:

'Do you suspect anyone else?'

'Was your father tough with him?'

'Papa was sad, crushed really. He never thought anything like this would happen to me. As far as he is concerned, I'm still his little girl.'

'Did he threaten Josset?'

'No. He's not that sort of person. He simply asked him what he intended to do, and straight away, of his own accord, Adrien started talking about divorce.'

'Did they argue? Were there raised voices?'

'Certainly not. I don't know how, but we ended up drinking a bottle of champagne between us. My father seemed to feel reassured. There was even a bit of a sparkle in his eyes that I wasn't used to seeing.'

'And after Adrien left?'

'We discussed the marriage. My father regretted that it

couldn't be a white wedding back in Fontenay, because people would talk.'

'Did he go on drinking?'

'He drained the bottle, which we hadn't finished before Adrien left.'

Her friend was keeping a close eye on her, to stop her saying too much.

'Did you take him back to his hotel?'

'I offered, but he declined.'

'Did your father seem overexcited, different from how he normally is?'

'No.'

'He is usually quite abstemious, unless I'm mistaken. Did you ever see him drink in Fontenay?'

'Never, except at dinner, when he'd have a little wine mixed with water. When he had to go to a café to meet someone, he always ordered a mineral water.'

'Yet he was drinking yesterday, before he came to see you unexpectedly.'

'Think before you answer,' warned Jeanine, with a knowing look.

'What should I say?'

'The truth,' Maigret replied.

'I believe he had one or two drinks while he was waiting.'

'Was he having difficulty forming his words?'

'He was slurring somewhat. That really struck me. But he was quite aware of what he was saying and doing.'

'Did you ring his hotel to make sure he had got back safely?'

'No. Why?'

'For his part, did he ring you this morning to say goodbye?'

'No. We never phone each other. We're not in the habit. Back home in Fontenay we don't have a telephone.'

Maigret decided not to pursue this.

'Thank you, mademoiselle.'

'What's he saying?' she asked, worried once more.

'Josset?'

'Yes.'

'He claims that he didn't kill his wife.'

'Do you believe him?'

'I'm not sure.'

'How is he? Does he need anything? He's not too down-hearted, is he?'

Her words were badly chosen, inadequate, out of proportion with the magnitude of the events.

'He is quite depressed. He spoke a lot about you.'

'Did he ask to see me?'

'That's for the examining magistrate to decide, not me.'

'Didn't he give you a message for me?'

'He didn't know I was coming to see you.'

'I suppose I'll be called in for questioning?'

'More than likely. But that depends on the magistrate too.'

'Can I continue to go to work?'

'I see no reason why not.'

It seemed a good moment to leave. As he went out through the main entrance, Maigret spotted the concierge, who was sitting eating opposite a man in shirt-sleeves, and she threw him a sarcastic look.

Perhaps it was Maigret's state of mind that made him see people and things in a disappointing light. He crossed the street and went into a little neighbourhood bar where there were four men playing belote and two others leaning on the bar chatting to the landlord.

He didn't know what he wanted, so ordered the first aperitif whose label he saw and sat there for a long time without speaking, frowning, in more or less the same place that Annette's father must have sat the previous evening.

By leaning forwards he could take in the whole of the house opposite, with the four pots of geraniums in one window. Jeanine, standing back in the shadows, had seen him cross the street and was talking to her friend, who was out of sight.

'You had a customer in here yesterday who stayed for a long time, is that right?'

The landlord picked up a newspaper and tapped his finger on the article about the Josset case.

'Do you mean the father?'

Then, turning to the others, he said:

'You know, I could tell there was something fishy about this from the start. First of all, he wasn't the sort of guy who propped up a bar for an hour at a time. He ordered a mineral water, and I was just about to pour it when he changed his mind.

'"You know what, I think I'll have . . ."

'He looked at the bottles but couldn't make his mind up.

'"A spirit . . . It doesn't matter which one."

'It's unusual for someone to order spirits at aperitif time.

'"Brandy? Calvados?"

'"A calvados please."

'It made him splutter. It was easy to see he wasn't used to drinking. He kept looking at the door across the street and the Métro exit further down. Two or three times I saw him moving his lips, as if he was talking to himself.'

The landlord paused and gave a frown.

'Aren't you Inspector Maigret?'

And as Maigret did not demur:

'Hey, you lot, look, it's the famous Inspector Maigret . . . So did that pharmacist confess? I've had my eye on that one too for a while. It's that car of his. You don't see many sports cars round here.

'I mainly used to see him in the mornings, when he came to pick up the girl. He would park at the edge of the pavement and look up. The young woman would wave to him from the window, then join him a few moments later.'

'How many glasses of calvados did your customer drink?'

'Four. Every time he ordered one he looked sheepish, as if he was worried we'd think he was a drunk.'

'Did he come back later on?'

'I didn't see him again. I saw the young woman this morning. She stood waiting for a while by the roadside, then headed off alone towards the Métro.'

Maigret paid for his drink, then walked in the direction of Place Clichy, keeping an eye out for a taxi. He found one free just as he was passing the top of Montmartre cemetery.

'Boulevard Richard-Lenoir.'

Nothing else happened that evening. He had dinner with his wife and made idle conversation. Familiar with his moods, she was careful not to ask him any questions.

Meanwhile, the investigation was taking its course. The cogs of the police machine kept turning, and the next morning Maigret found a certain number of reports on his desk.

Contrary to his normal practice, and for no obvious reason, he was going to compile a sort of personal file of this case.

The chronology in particular seemed important, and he set about reconstructing the chain of events, hour by hour.

As the crime had been uncovered in the morning, or more exactly in the small hours, the early newspapers hadn't mentioned it; it was the radio that had first announced the dramatic events in Rue Lopert.

At the time the radio broadcast was going out the journalists were positioned outside the Josset residence in Auteuil, where the men from the public prosecutor's office had arrived.

Between midday and one o'clock the first editions of the afternoon papers spoke about the event, albeit in brief terms.

Only one of the dailies, tipped off by the concierge in Rue Caulaincourt, printed the story of Duché's visit to his daughter and his encounter with Annette's lover in its third edition.

Meanwhile, the town clerk was on a train heading back to Fontenay-le-Comte, out of reach of any fresh news.

Later, they would track down one of his travelling companions, a grain merchant from the Niort area. The two men didn't know each other. On leaving Paris, the compartment was full, but after Poitiers it was just the two of them.

'I thought I knew him by sight. I couldn't for the life of me remember where we had met, but I gave him a discreet nod of recognition anyway. He responded with a surprised, almost suspicious look and huddled into his corner.

'He seemed out of sorts. His eyes were puffy, as if he hadn't slept all night. At Poitiers he went to the buffet for a bottle of water, which he gulped down.'

'Was he reading?'

'No. He was just idly watching the landscape go by. At times his eyes closed, and then finally he fell asleep . . . When I got home, I suddenly remembered where I had seen him before: in the sub-préfecture at Fontenay, where I had to go to sign some papers.'

Maigret, who had travelled specifically to meet the grain merchant – his name was Lousteau – made an effort to get more out of him. It was as if he was chasing an idea he couldn't express.

'Did you notice his clothes?'

'I couldn't tell you what colour they were; just dark, rather cheap.'

'Were they crumpled, as if he had been sleeping rough?'

'I didn't pay any attention to that. I was mainly looking at his face. Hold on . . . There was a raincoat in the luggage rack, on top of his case.'

It had taken a bit of time to locate the hotel where

Annette's father had stayed, the Hôtel de la Reine et de Poitiers near Gare d'Austerlitz.

It was a second-rate hotel, dimly lit and a bit run-down but respectable, with a regular clientele. Martin Duché had stayed there a few times. His previous visit had been two years earlier, when he had brought his daughter to Paris.

'He stayed in number 53. He didn't take any meals at the hotel. He arrived on Tuesday on the 15.53 train and then went out again as soon as he had filled in his registration form, saying that he was only going to stay one night.'

'What time did he get back in the evening?'

At this point they drew a blank. The night clerk, who had his camp bed set up in the office, was a Czech who spoke only a little French and who had been committed to Sainte-Anne psychiatric hospital on two occasions. The name Duché didn't ring a bell; nor did his description. When room 53 was mentioned, he looked at the key board and scratched his head.

'He comes, he goes, he comes back, he goes . . .' he muttered irritably.

'What time did you go to bed?'

'Not before midnight. I always lock up and go to bed at midnight. That's orders . . .'

'Do you know if number 53 had returned?'

The poor man did what he could, but what he could didn't amount to very much. He wasn't working at the hotel two years earlier, when Duché had last visited.

They showed him a photograph.

'Who's this?' he asked, anxious to please the people who were asking him questions.

Maigret had obstinately gone as far as finding the people who had stayed in the rooms on either side of number 53. One lived in Marseille and was on the telephone.

'I don't know anything. I got back at eleven and I didn't hear a thing.'

'Were you alone?'

'Of course.'

The man was married. He had come to Paris without his wife. And it was almost certain that he hadn't spent the night on his own.

As for number 51, that was a Belgian who was just passing through France who proved impossible to trace.

In any case, at 7.45 in the morning, Duché had been in his room and had rung down to order his breakfast. The maid hadn't noticed anything out of the ordinary, except that the guest had ordered a triple coffee.

'He seemed tired . . .'

It was all a bit vague. It was impossible to get any more out of her. At 8.30, without taking a bath, Duché had come downstairs and paid his bill to the cashier, who knew him.

'He was much as he normally was. I've never seen him look happy. He never seemed to be in good health. He would sometimes stop as if he was listening to his own heartbeat. I knew another one like him, a good customer who came every month. He had the same look about him, behaved in the same way, and one morning he dropped dead on the staircase without even managing to call for help . . .'

Duché had taken his train. He was on it, sitting opposite the grain merchant, as Maigret was questioning Josset at Quai des Orfèvres.

At the same time a reporter from a morning newspaper, after hurrying round to Rue Caulaincourt, was calling his correspondent in Fontenay-le-Comte.

The concierge had not told Maigret about this visit by the journalist, to whom she gave the name and address of Annette's father.

These small details were all jumbled together, and it required time and patience to derive a more or less coherent picture from them.

As the train drew into the station at Fontenay-le-Comte that afternoon, Martin Duché was still unaware of what had happened. So were the people of Fontenay, as the radio had not yet given out the name of their fellow citizen, and it was only through guesswork that they could have made a connection between the chief clerk at the sub-préfecture and the drama in Rue Lopert.

Only the newspaper correspondent knew what was going on. He had alerted a photographer. They were both waiting on the platform, and as Duché got out of the train he was surprised to be greeted by a flashbulb.

'If we could have a word with you, Monsieur Duché . . .'

He blinked, bewildered and confused.

'I guess you haven't heard the news yet?'

The reporter stated categorically that the town clerk had seemed like a man who had no idea what had hit him. Suitcase in hand and raincoat draped over his arm, he made his way to the exit and handed his ticket to the station guard, who touched his cap in greeting. The photographer took another picture. The reporter stuck close to Annette's father.

The three of them came out into a sunlit Rue de la République.

'Madame Josset was murdered last night . . .'

The journalist, whose name was Pecqueur, had a round face and chubby cheeks, and the same protuberant blue eyes as Annette. He was redheaded and shabbily dressed and smoked an overly large pipe to give himself a certain gravitas.

Maigret interviewed him too, in the back room of the Café de la Poste, next to an unused billiard table.

'How did he react?'

'He came to a halt and looked me in the eyes as if he thought I was trying to catch him out.'

'Catch him out?'

'No one in Fontenay knew that his daughter was involved with a married man. He must have thought I had found out and was trying to get him to talk about it.'

'What did he say?'

'After a pause, he said in a hard voice:

'"I don't know Madame Josset."

'So I told him that my paper would be talking about it in the morning and would be giving all the details of the case. I added that I had just heard about it by telephone:

'"An evening paper has already run a piece on your meeting with your daughter and Adrien Josset in Rue Caulaincourt."'

Maigret asked:

'Did you know him well?'

'As well as anyone in Fontenay, from having seen him at the préfecture and around town.'

'Did he ever stop suddenly when he was walking around?'

'Well, at shop windows, yes.'

'Was he ill?'

'I've no idea. He lived alone, he didn't go to cafés and he didn't speak much.'

'Did you manage to get the interview you were after?'

'He carried on walking in silence. I asked him anything that came into my head:

'"Do you think Josset killed his wife?"

'"Is it true that he intended to marry your daughter?"

'But he remained surly and just ignored me. On two or three occasions he growled:

'"I've got nothing to say."

'"Yet you did meet Adrien Josset?"

'"I've got nothing to say."

'We reached the bridge. He turned left along the riverbank, where he lives in a little brick house that is looked after by a cleaning lady. I took a photo of the house, as the paper never has enough photographs.'

'Was the cleaning lady there?'

'No. She only worked in the mornings.'

'Who cooked his meals?'

'He normally had lunch at the Trois Pigeons. He cooked his own dinner in the evening.'

'Did he ever go out?'

'Rarely. Once a week he went to the cinema.'

'On his own?'

'Yes, always.'

'Did anyone hear anything that evening, or during the night?'

'No. A cyclist who was passing at one in the morning noticed a light on, that's all. The next morning, when the cleaning lady arrived, the light was still burning.'

Martin Duché had not undressed, had not eaten anything. Nothing was out of place in the house.

As far as it is possible to reconstitute the sequence of events, he had gone to get a photo album from a drawer in the kitchen. The first few pages contained faded portraits of his parents and his wife, one of him in his gunner's uniform when he did his military service, a wedding photo, baby pictures of Annette on a bearskin rug, some of her at five, at ten, at her first communion, then in a class photo at the convent school she attended.

The album, open at this page, was lying on a side table in front of an armchair.

How long had Duché sat there before he made his mind up? He must have gone up to his bedroom on the first floor to fetch his revolver from the night table, which he had left open.

He had come back downstairs, sat down in the armchair again and put a bullet in his head.

The next morning, the newspaper headlines announced:

THE JOSSET CASE CLAIMS ITS SECOND VICTIM

In the minds of the readers it was as if Josset had killed Annette's father himself.

There was talk about his years as a widower, his

dignified, solitary life, his love for his only daughter, the shock he had received when he went to her apartment in Rue Caulaincourt and learned of the relationship between Annette and her employer.

Josset was already a condemned man. Even Coméliau, who should have seen things from a purely professional point of view, was quite wound up as he spoke to Maigret on the telephone.

'Have you read this?'

It was Thursday morning. Maigret had just arrived at work, having read the newspapers standing up on the bus.

'I hope Josset has found a lawyer, because I am going to summon him to my chambers and bring this to a swift conclusion . . . The public won't accept this being dragged out any longer . . .'

That meant that Maigret could say nothing more. The examining magistrate was taking the matter in hand, and the inspector, in theory, could only act under his instructions from now on.

Perhaps he wouldn't see Josset again, except in court. And he would know only what the magistrate deemed fit to tell him about any further interrogations.

That couldn't have been the day he went to Niort and Fontenay, because Coméliau wouldn't have failed to hear about it and given him a stern reprimand.

According to regulations, he wasn't allowed the shortest excursion outside of Paris.

Even his first telephone call to Doctor Liorant, who lived in Rue Rabelais in Fontenay-le-Comte and whom he had met previously in the town, hadn't strictly been by the book.

'Maigret here . . . Do you remember me, doctor?'

The reply was cool, cautious, and this immediately set Maigret on alert.

'Could I pick your brains, in a personal capacity?'

'I'm listening.'

'I was wondering whether Martin Duché was, by chance, one of your patients.'

Silence.

'I don't imagine that is in breach of patient confidentiality.'

'He did have reason to come to see me.'

'Was he seriously ill?'

'I'm afraid I can't tell you that.'

'Just a moment, doctor . . . Forgive me for insisting, but a man's life is at stake. I have been told that Duché would come to a sudden halt, in the street or somewhere else, like someone suffering from angina.'

'Was it a doctor who told you that? If that's so, he was wrong to do so.'

'It wasn't a doctor.'

'In that case, it is merely unfounded speculation.'

'Can't you tell me whether his life was in danger?'

'I have absolutely nothing to add. If you will excuse me, inspector, I have a dozen patients waiting.'

Maigret would see him again, no more successfully, on his trip to Niort and Fontenay, while between trains, out of sight of Coméliau and even of Quai des Orfèvres.

6. The Old Insomniac

Rarely had spring been so radiant. The newspapers were vying with each other to announce record temperatures and an unbroken spell of dry weather. Rarely, too, at Quai des Orfèvres, had Maigret seemed so sombre and touchy. It got to the point where those who weren't in the know began to express concern about his wife's health.

Coméliau had seized the initiative and applied the letter of the law, more or less spiriting Josset away, with the result that Maigret did not even have the opportunity to speak to him again.

Every day, or almost, the drug manufacturer was brought from the Santé prison to the examining magistrate's chambers, where his lawyer, Maître Lenain, awaited him.

He was not a good choice. If Maigret had been able, he would have advised against his appointment. Lenain was one of the three or four leading lights of the bar. He specialized in high-profile trials and once he took on a spectacular case he filled as many column inches in the newspapers as a film star.

The reporters hung on his almost daily pronouncements, his rather cutting, off-the-cuff remarks. Because he had brought off two or three acquittals that were thought impossible he was known as the counsel for lost causes.

Following these interrogations, Maigret would be

handed baffling orders by Coméliau, usually without any explanation: witnesses to chase up, details to be checked, tasks all the more irksome because they seemed to bear very little relation to the crime in Rue Lopert.

The magistrate wasn't doing this out of personal animosity. Even though Coméliau had always distrusted Maigret and his methods, that had more to do with the gulf between their ways of seeing things than anything else.

In the end it boiled down to social class. The magistrate had remained a man of his milieu even as the world changed around him. His grandfather had been president of the Court of Appeal in Paris, and his father still sat on the State Council, while one of his uncles was the French ambassador in Helsinki.

He himself had studied for a career in the State Audit Office, and it was only when he had failed the entrance exam that he had become a magistrate.

He was very much a product of his background, a slave to its customs, its rules for living, even its language.

One might have expected his hands-on experience at the Palais de Justice would have given him a more nuanced view of humanity, but that wasn't the case, and in the end he invariably adopted the default viewpoint of his social milieu.

In his eyes, Josset was, if not a born criminal, definitely the guilty type. Hadn't he risen under false pretences to a class that was not his own, firstly through an illicit affair, then by an unsuitable marriage? Didn't his affair with Annette and his promise to marry her simply confirm that view?

On the other hand, the young woman's father, Martin Duché, who had chosen to take his own life rather than face disgrace, was a man after Coméliau's own flinty heart. He was the epitome of the traditional honest servant: modest, self-effacing, inconsolable after the death of his wife.

That he had been drinking on the evening of Rue Caulaincourt was a matter of no importance to Coméliau. To Maigret, it was a telling detail.

Maigret would have sworn that Annette's father had been ill for a long time, and that his condition was probably incurable.

And wasn't his so-called dignity based on nothing more than pride?

He had returned to Fontenay feeling somewhat queasy and ashamed, deep down, about the way he had behaved the previous evening. Then, far from finding peace and quiet, he was no sooner off the train before he was accosted by a journalist and a photographer.

That bothered Maigret, as did the attitude of Doctor Liorant. He promised himself he would revisit this, try to flush the matter out into the open, even though his hands were tied.

His men had traipsed all over Paris, checking facts, and Maigret himself had established a chronology of Josset's movements on the night of the crime, though he didn't realize yet how important that chronology would turn out to be.

In his sole interrogation at police headquarters Josset had claimed that, after he left Rue Caulaincourt around

8.30, he had driven around at random before stopping at a bar in the vicinity of Place de la République.

They had located the bar, La Bonne Chope, Boulevard du Temple, where one of the waiters remembered him. As there was a customer who turned up every evening on the dot of nine and he hadn't yet arrived, Josset's arrival in Rue du Temple could be pinned down to between 8.45 and nine o'clock. That all added up.

At the Select on the Champs-Élysées it was even easier, as the barman, Jean, had known the drug manufacturer for years.

'He came in at nine and ordered a whisky.'

'Was that what he normally drank?'

'No, his usual tipple was champagne. When he walked in I even reached for the ice bucket, where we always have a bottle chilling.'

'Did anything strike you about his behaviour?'

'He downed his drink in one go and handed me his glass for a refill. He didn't talk but just looked straight ahead. I asked him:

'"Everything OK, Monsieur Josset?"

'"Not so good," he replied.

'He said something about some meal that had disagreed with him, and I offered him some bicarbonate of soda.

'He turned it down and had a third drink before he left, still looking like he had something on his mind.'

The details still matched.

In Josset's own account, he had then headed off towards Rue Lopert, where he had arrived at 10.05.

Torrence had questioned everyone in the street. At this

time of day most of the buildings had their shutters closed. A neighbour had come home at 10.15 and not noticed anything.

'Were there any cars parked outside the Josset building?'

'I think so. The big one was there, at least.'

'And the small one?'

'I couldn't say.'

'Did you notice any lights on in the building?'

'I believe so . . . but I couldn't swear to it.'

Only the owner of the house opposite was certain, so certain that Torrence had repeated the questions three or four times and written down the replies word for word.

This was one François Lalinde, aged seventy-six, a former colonial administrator, now retired for a number of years. No longer in good health, prone to recurrent bouts of fever, he never left his house, where he lived with a coloured maid he had brought back from Africa, whom he called Julie.

He stated that, as was his custom, he hadn't gone to bed before four o'clock in the morning and had spent the early part of the night in his armchair near the window.

He had shown Torrence the chair. It was on the first floor, in a room that served as a bedroom, library, living room and junk room all in one. It was the only room in the house he really occupied, and he more or less never left it, except to go to the adjacent bathroom.

He was a bad-tempered, impatient man who didn't tolerate being contradicted.

'Do you know your neighbours opposite?'

'By sight, inspector, by sight!'

He kept grinning, and there was something menacing in the way he smiled.

'Those people have chosen to live their lives in full view of everyone. They don't even have the basic decency to have shutters on their windows.'

He made it clear that he knew a lot more than he was letting on.

'A crazy way to live!'

'Who are you talking about?'

'Both of them. The woman as well as the man . . . The servants aren't any better.'

'Did you see Josset come home on Tuesday evening?'

'How could I not see him, since I was sitting in front of the window?'

'Did you do anything except look at what was happening in the street?'

'I read. Every time I heard a noise it gave me a start. I hate noise, especially the noise of cars.'

'Did you hear any cars pull up outside the Josset house?'

'Yes, and I gave a jump, as always. I regard noise as a personal assault.'

'So you heard Monsieur Josset's car arrive, and then, no doubt, the car door being closed?'

'The car door, yes, that's right, young man.'

'Did you look outside?'

'I did, and I saw him returning home.'

'Did you have a wristwatch?'

'No. There is a clock on the wall just opposite my chair, as you can verify for yourself. It never loses more than three minutes a month.'

'What time was it?'

'Ten forty-five.'

Torrence, like all of Maigret's team, had read the transcript of Josset's interrogation and had insisted:

'Are you sure it wasn't five past ten?'

'I'm certain. I am always very precise, have been all my life.'

'In the evening or during the night, do you ever fall asleep in your chair?'

This time, Monsieur Lalinde lost his temper, and poor Torrence had an almighty struggle to get him to calm down again. The old man would not allow himself to be contradicted, especially on this subject, as he took great pride in being a man who never slept.

'You recognized Monsieur Josset?'

'Who else could it have been?'

'I asked you if you recognized him.'

'Of course.'

'Could you make out his face?'

'There's a streetlamp nearby, and there was a full moon.'

'At this moment were there any lights on inside the house?'

'No, sir.'

'Not even in the maid's room?'

'The maid had gone to bed half an hour earlier.'

'How do you know?'

'Because I saw her close her window, and the light went out straight afterwards.'

'What time?'

'A quarter past ten.'

'Did Monsieur Josset turn on a light on the ground floor?'

'I'm sure he did.'

'Do you remember seeing the ground floor lit up after he went in?'

'Perfectly.'

'Then?'

'Then it was just the same as normal. The ground floor went dark and the lights came on on the first floor.'

'In which room?'

Both Josset's room and his wife's room looked on to the street: Josset's on the right, Christine's on the left.

'Both.'

'Could you see anything going on inside the house?'

'No. That was of no interest to me.'

'Could you see through the curtains?'

'Only a shadow whenever someone walked between a lamp and the window.'

'You didn't look even for a short while?'

'I buried my nose in my book.'

'Until when?'

'Until I heard the door across the street open and close again.'

'What time was that?'

'Eleven forty.'

'Did you hear a car engine?'

'No. The man set off on foot towards the Auteuil church, carrying a suitcase.'

'Were there any lights on in the house?'

'No.'

Hitherto, they had been using the chronology Josset had supplied to Maigret. From now onwards there was no shortage of witnesses. They had located the driver of the 403 which was parked in front of the Auteuil church, a man called Brugnali.

'The customer hired me at half past midnight. I noted down the route in my logbook. He was carrying a suitcase, and I took him to Avenue Marceau.'

'How was he?'

'Completely drunk and he reeked of booze. Because he had a case with him, I asked him which station he wanted.'

In Avenue Marceau, Josset paid his fare and headed towards a large town-house which had a brass plate to the left of the door.

They had also found the second taxi, the one Josset had taken when he left his office.

The cabaret he had visited at 1.30 was a small bar called Le Parc aux Cerfs. The doorman and the barman remembered him.

'He didn't want a table. He seemed a bit surprised to find himself here, and his jaw dropped when he saw Ninouche doing her striptease. Ninouche was just getting to the end of her first show, so I can be sure what time it was. He drank a whisky and bought one for Marina, one of our hostesses, but didn't pay her any attention.'

During this time, the taxi-driver was outside, talking to another driver who was working in cahoots with the doorman to stop him parking there.

'Go and get your money, and I'll take your customer when he comes out.'

But Josset's arrival had put an end to the argument, and the same taxi in which he had left his case took him back to Rue Lopert. Even though he was familiar with the neighbourhood, the driver had managed to do a whole circuit before Josset had shown him the best route.

'It was around one forty-five, maybe one fifty, when I dropped him off.'

'How was he?'

'Drunker than on the way there.'

Lalinde, the former colonial administrator, corroborated the time of return. The lights were turned on once again.

'On the ground floor?'

'Of course. Then on the first floor.'

'In both rooms?'

'And in the bathroom, which has a frosted-glass window.'

'Did Josset go out again?'

'At two thirty, turning out the lights when he left.'

'Did he take his car?'

'No. And this time he headed for Rue Chardon-Lagache with a package under his arm.'

'What size of package?'

'Quite big, more long than wide.'

'Thirty, forty centimetres in length?'

'I'd say nearer forty.'

'How wide?'

'I'd say about twenty.'

'Didn't you go to bed then?'

'No. I was still awake at three forty-eight exactly when

a police van came to a screeching halt and a half-dozen police officers jumped out and went inside the house.'

'If I've got this right, during the whole evening and night you never left your chair?'

'Not until four thirty, when I went to bed.'

'Did you hear anything after that?'

'The sound of cars coming and going.'

Here, too, the various accounts matched up, as Josset had arrived at the Auteuil police station around three thirty, and they had sent the van to Rue Lopert a few minutes later, just as he was starting to make his statement.

Maigret had passed on this report to Coméliau. A little later, the magistrate had asked him to drop by his chambers, where he was alone.

'Have you read this?'

'Of course.'

'Did anything strike you about it?'

'One detail, which I hope to discuss with you later.'

'What strikes me is that Josset told the truth about most things – things not directly related to the crime itself. His chronology is spot on for most of the night.

'But where he makes out that he went back at five past ten at the latest, Monsieur Lalinde saw him arrive at ten forty-five.

'So he wasn't asleep on the ground floor, as he claims.

'He was up on the first floor at ten forty-five, and the lights were on *in both rooms*.

'Note that this time corresponds to what Doctor Paul considers the likely time of the crime. What do you say to that?'

'I'd simply like to make an observation. According to

With a range of different subtitles:

JOSSET, BACK TO THE WALL, GOES ON THE ATTACK

And:

THE DEFENCE'S DESPERATE LAST THROW OF THE DICE

Coméliau, as was his wont, had refused to make any statement and remained ensconced in his chambers.

Lenain, as was *his* wont, had not only read out a written statement to the journalists, but, once his client had been led away by two policemen, had held what was to all intents and purposes a press conference in the corridors of the Palais.

The statement was short and sweet:

Until now, Adrien Josset, who stands accused of the murder of his wife, has maintained a chivalrous silence concerning her private life and secret behaviour.

Seeing as the case is about to be passed on to the Grand Jury, he has reluctantly decided, on the advice of his counsel, to raise a corner of this veil of secrecy. As a result, the investigation will take a new direction.

It will reveal that any one of a number of people could have killed Christine Josset, about whom little has been said to date, so concerted has been the effort to condemn her husband.

Maigret would have liked to know what had led up to this decision, to be informed about the conversations that had taken place between the two men, the lawyer and his client, in his cell at the Santé prison.

It reminded him a little of the scene in Rue Caulaincourt. Annette's father had come in and had hardly said a word. He had simply asked:

'What are you planning to do?'

And straight away, Josset, who hid behind Monsieur Jules when it came to letting an employee go, had promised to divorce his wife in order to marry the girl.

A skilful and unscrupulous operator like Lenain could probably get him to say whatever he wanted.

Of course, the reporters had bombarded the lawyer with questions.

'Are you saying Madame Josset had a lover?'

The lawyer smiled enigmatically.

'No, gentlemen, not a lover.'

'Lovers plural?'

'It's not as simple as that; that in itself wouldn't explain anything.'

They didn't follow. Only he knew where he was going with this.

'Madame Josset – and, I hasten to add, she was perfectly entitled to this – had a string of protégés. Her friends, yes, her friends will confirm this; indeed, in some circles these protégés were talked about in much the same way as the racehorses of such and such an owner.'

He went on in his self-satisfied way:

'When she was very young she married a very famous

man, Sir Austin Lowell, who educated her in the ways of the world . . . The world of the powerful, of those who pull the strings. At the start she was, like many others in her situation, little more than an ornament.

'Let me be clear: she was not Austin Lowell. She was the attractive Madame Lowell, whom he dressed, covered in jewels, displayed at race-courses, premières, cabarets and salons.

'When she was widowed at the age of thirty, she wanted to carry on, but *on her own terms*, if I might put it that way.

'She had no intention of continuing to be the subordinate half of a couple, the ornamental accessory; she was going to be top dog.

'That is why, instead of marrying a man of her class, which she could have done easily, she went and found Josset behind the counter of a pharmacy.

'She wanted her chance to be in charge, to have someone by her side who owed her everything, who would be her possession.

'She discovered, however, that the young pharmacy assistant was a much stronger character than she had imagined.

'He made such a success of his pharmaceutical business that he became a personality in his own right.

'And that is it. That's the root of the drama.

'She grew older and began to dread the moment when she would no longer be the object of male attention—'

'Excuse me,' a journalist butted in. 'Did she already have lovers?'

'Suffice it to say that she has never lived according to

bourgeois norms. The day came when, no longer able to dominate her husband, she sought others to dominate.

'They are those I referred to earlier as her protégés – and that is a word she chose herself and by all accounts pronounced with a satisfied smile.

'And there were many of them. We are familiar with some of them. There have certainly been others we know nothing about but whom, I hope, our investigation will uncover.

'Mostly they were unknown artists, painters, musicians, singers, whom she met God knows where and whom she seemed determined to launch on their careers.

'I can name one quite well-known cabaret singer, still around today, who owes his success entirely to a fortuitous encounter with Madame Josset in the garage where he worked as a mechanic.

'For all those who achieved success, there were many who were revealed to be talentless, and after a few weeks or months she dropped them.

'Need I add that these young people didn't always take too kindly to being dumped back into obscurity?

'She had introduced them to her friends as rising stars of the theatre, the art world or the cinema. She had dressed them in fine clothes, found them decent places to live. They had lived in her shadow, in her slipstream.

'Then they would wake up one morning and find they were nobody again.'

'Can you name names?'

'I will leave that to the examining magistrate. I gave him a list of names which no doubt includes many fine young men. We are not accusing anyone. All we are saying is that there are a certain number of people who had reasons to want Christine Josset—'

'Anyone in particular?'

'It would be a good idea to begin searching among her most recent protégés.'

Maigret had thought about this. From the start he had considered looking into the private life of the victim and her entourage.

Up until now, he had hit a brick wall. And again, as in the case of Coméliau, it was to do with class, even caste.

Christine Josset circulated in an even more narrow world than the examining magistrate, a handful of individuals whose names appeared in the papers, whose every move was chronicled, who were the subject of fanciful stories and yet about whom the general public knew next to nothing in reality.

Maigret was still only a junior inspector when he had made a remark about this, one often repeated to novices at Quai des Orfèvres. Ordered to conduct the surveillance of a banker – one who would be arrested a few months later – he had said to his chief:

'To properly understand how his mind works I should eat soft-boiled eggs and croissants with financiers every morning.'

Doesn't every social class have its own language, taboos, moral permissiveness?

Whenever he asked, 'What do you think of Madame Josset?' he was invariably told:

'Christine? Why, she is simply *adorable*.' In her own

milieu, she was no Josset, she was *Christine*. 'She's interested in everything, passionate, in love with life . . .'

'And her husband?'

'A fine fellow . . .'

But this was said more coldly, which showed that Josset, for all his success in business, had never been fully adopted by his wife's friends.

He was tolerated, in the way that the mistress or wife of a famous man is tolerated:

'Well, it's up to him if he likes . . .'

Coméliau must be furious. He would be even more so once he had read all the papers. He had built a case he was satisfied with and was about to send to the Grand Jury.

Now the investigation had to start all over again. It was not possible simply to ignore Lenain's accusations, especially as he had made sure to give them maximum publicity.

It was no longer a matter of questioning concierges, taxi-drivers and neighbours in Rue Lopert.

It was necessary to engage with a whole new milieu, to elicit confidences, names, to draw up a list of these already notorious protégés, and it would no doubt be Maigret's task to check their alibis.

A journalist raised an objection:

'Josset claimed to have gone to sleep on the ground floor, in an armchair, when he got home at five past ten. A reliable witness, who lives in the house opposite, claims that he didn't get home until ten forty-five.'

'A reliable witness can make a mistake,' the lawyer retorted. 'Monsieur Lalinde, the man you are referring to, no doubt did see a man enter the house at ten forty-five, while my client was sleeping.'

'And that would be the killer?'

'Probably.'

'And he managed to get past Josset without being seen?'

'There were no lights on on the ground floor. The more I think about it, the more I am sure that at the time of the murder there were not two, but three cars parked outside the house. I went to check the scene itself. I didn't manage to get inside Monsieur Lalinde's house, as his maid was far from welcoming. But I would argue nevertheless that, from this worthy old gentleman's window, it is possible to see the Cadillac and any car parked in front of it, but *not a car standing behind*. I have asked for this hypothesis to be checked out. If I am right, I am prepared to swear that there were three cars there.'

Madame Maigret was very worked up that evening. She had resisted so far, but now she had become deeply engrossed in this case that was the talk of the town.

'Do you think Lenain was right to go on the offensive?'

'No.'

'Is Josset innocent?'

He looked at her without really seeing her.

'I'd say it's fifty-fifty.'

'Will he be found guilty?'

'Very likely, especially now.'

'Can't you do anything?'

This time, he simply shrugged his shoulders.

7. Monsieur Jules and the Chairwoman

Maigret witnessed, unable to intervene, a phenomenon he had observed several times before, one which never failed to make an impression on him. His old comrade Lombras, the commissioner of the Municipal Police, who was responsible for controlling crowds and demonstrations on the city's streets, would often say that Paris, just like a person, sometimes 'got out of bed on the wrong side' and started the day in a bad mood, ready to fly off the handle at the slightest provocation.

It can be a bit like that in criminal cases. A cold-blooded murder carried out in the foulest of circumstances might pass by unnoticed, the investigation and then the trial playing out against a backdrop of public indifference, if not indulgence.

Then, for no apparent reason, a quite mundane crime can incite public indignation, without anyone being able to work out why.

There was no organized campaign. There was no one behind the scenes, as those who think they are well informed like to say, orchestrating a campaign against Josset.

Of course, the papers had talked a lot about the case and continued to do so, but the papers merely reflect public opinion and provide their readers with what they ask for.

Why had everyone been against Josset from the very start?

One reason was the twenty-three stab wounds. When a murderer loses his head and continues stabbing a corpse he is regarded as a savage. The psychiatrists might see this as a sign of diminished responsibility, but the public at large consider it rather as an aggravating circumstance.

Of the various characters in this drama, Josset had from the start been the villain that everyone loved to hate, and perhaps there was an explanation for that too. Even those who had never seen him had picked up from all the press coverage that he was weak and spineless, and such cowardice is not easily forgiven.

Equally unforgivable is denial of the facts, and as far as most people were concerned Josset's guilt was a copper-bottomed fact.

If he had confessed, if he had claimed it was a crime of passion, a mental aberration, and asked for forgiveness with the appropriate remorse, most would have been willing to show some leniency.

But instead he chose to defy *logic* and *good sense*, which seemed like an insult to the intelligence of the public.

As early as Tuesday, when he was interrogating him, Maigret had seen this coming. Coméliau's reactions were a giveaway. The early headlines of the afternoon papers were another.

Since then the antipathy had only grown more acute, and it was rare to hear anyone doubt Josset's guilt or at least offer, if not excuses, then attenuating circumstances.

Martin Duché's suicide had capped off the disaster, as Josset was held responsible not only for one death, but for two.

Finally, his lawyer, Maître Lenain, had fanned the flames with his ill-judged comments and accusations.

It was difficult in such conditions to question witnesses properly. Even the most honest ones, totally in good faith, tended to remember only those things that worked against the interests of the accused.

In the end, Josset was simply unlucky. When it came to the knife, for example, he said he had thrown it in the Seine from the middle of Pont Mirabeau. Since Wednesday a diver had been scouring the mud for hours, watched by hundreds of onlookers leaning over the parapet, while photographers and even TV crews sprang into action every time the large brass-helmeted head emerged from the water.

But the diver had come up from each dive empty-handed and the next day had continued searching with no further success.

For those familiar with the riverbed of the Seine, this wasn't surprising. Next to the pillars of the bridge the current is quite strong and it forms undertows that can carry even a quite heavy object some distance away.

In other places the mud is quite thick, and any detritus sinks deeply into it.

Josset had been unable to point out the exact spot where he had stood, which is understandable, given the state of mind he said he was in.

For the public, however, this was proof that he had been

lying. He was accused, for some unknown reason, of hiding the weapon somewhere else. It wasn't just a matter of the dagger. Monsieur Lalinde, the former colonial administrator, whose word no one doubted, whom no one dared to call a senile or at least addled old man, had described a package of some bulk, whose dimensions were far larger than those of a commando knife.

What could this package that he carried away from the scene have contained?

Even a discovery that initially seemed to aid the prisoner, and about which his lawyer was prematurely triumphant, ended up working against him.

Criminal Records had lifted a certain number of fingerprints from the house in Rue Lopert, which was now known as the glass house because of its futuristic architecture. These prints, classified by category, had been compared with those of Josset, his wife, the two servants and a man from the gas board who had come to read the meter on the Monday afternoon, a few hours before the murder.

But some prints remained unidentified. They were found on the banister of the stairway and, more abundantly, in the victim's room and that of her husband.

They were the prints of a man with a large thumb which had a very characteristic small, round scar.

When she was questioned about this, Madame Siran stated that neither Madame Josset nor her husband had received a visitor in the previous few days; nor, to her knowledge, had any stranger gone upstairs to the bedrooms.

Carlotta, who remained on duty in the evenings after the cook had gone home, corroborated this.

In the newspapers this was presented as:

A MYSTERY VISITOR?

Of course, Maître Lenain made a big fuss about this discovery, and he started to build a whole line of defence on it.

According to him, Doctor Paul could have committed an error of judgement. There is no reason, said the lawyer, why the murder could not have taken place a bit before ten o'clock, that is, before Josset got to Rue Lopert.

Even if the medical examiner was right, there was no justification in rejecting the hypothesis that a stranger could have got into the house while Josset, who had been drinking heavily, was fast asleep in a chair on the ground floor, where no lights were on.

Lenain had managed to conduct an experiment in the same location at the same time. He had sat in the chair in which Christine's husband had sat, and six unsuspecting individuals had been asked to walk one after the other through the dark room to the staircase. Only two of them had noticed someone sitting there.

The objection to this was that the moon had not been in the same position on the night of the crime and that the sky was overcast.

And besides, Lalinde refused to change a single word of his initial statement.

It was Maigret who received a visit from the

upholsterer. He had read the papers with some concern and had come into Quai des Orfèvres to tell them what he knew. He frequently did work for the Jossets. He was the one who, a few years earlier, had put up their curtains and wallpaper. A few months earlier he had changed some of the curtains, including those in Madame Josset's room, which had been refurnished.

'The servants seem to have forgotten that I was there,' he said. 'They mentioned the gasman but not me. Three days ago I had to go to Rue Lopert because Madame Josset had told me that the curtain cords had come loose. It is not unusual. I happened to be in the area on Monday around three o'clock so I dropped by.'

'What did you see?'

'Madame Siran answered the door to me. She didn't come up with me as she hates stairs and she knew that I was familiar with the house.'

'Were you on your own?'

'Yes, I'd left my colleague on another job in Avenue Versailles. My work took only a few minutes.'

'Did you see the maid?'

'She came into the room briefly while I was working, and I said hello.'

Neither of the two women had remembered the upholsterer when they were questioned.

Maigret led the man up to Criminal Records. They took his fingerprints, which were a perfect match for the prints of the famous mystery visitor.

The next day, it was Maigret once more who received the anonymous letter that would stoke public indignation.

It was a sheet of paper torn from a school exercise book, folded in quarters and stuffed inside a cheap envelope stained with grease marks, as if it had been written on a kitchen table.

The postmark showed the eighteenth arrondissement, where Annette Duché lived.

If Detective Chief Inspector Maigret thinks he's so clever, he should go and question a certain Hortense Malletier, in Rue Lepic, a backstreet abortionist. The Duché girl visited three months ago along with her lover.

At this stage in proceedings, Maigret preferred to take the note to Coméliau in person.

'Read it.'

The examining magistrate read the letter twice.

'Have you checked?'

'I didn't want to do anything without your instructions.'

'It would be best if you went to see this Hortense Malletier yourself. Is she in your files?'

Maigret had already consulted the Vice Squad's most recent lists.

'She was arrested once, ten years ago, but nothing was proved.'

The Malletier woman lived on the fifth floor of an old building near the Moulin de la Galette. She was in her sixties and suffered from dropsy. She wore felt slippers and could only walk around with the help of a cane. There was a stifling smell in her apartment, and in a large cage by the window there were a dozen or so canaries.

'What do the police want with me? I haven't done anything. I'm just a poor old woman who is no trouble to anyone.'

Her pale face was framed by grey hair, so thin on top that her scalp was exposed.

First, Maigret showed her a photo of Annette Duché.

'Do you recognize her?'

'Her face is all over the papers.'

'Did she come to see you about three months ago?'

'Why would she come and see me? I haven't read the cards for ages.'

'So you read cards too?'

'So what? Everyone has to make a living somehow.'

'She found herself pregnant, but after seeing you, she wasn't any more.'

'Who made that up? It's a complete lie!'

Janvier, who had accompanied his chief, searched all the drawers but found nothing, as Maigret had expected.

'It's important that we know what really happened. She didn't come on her own. There was a man with her.'

'It's been years since a man set foot in my apartment.'

She stuck to her guns. She knew the score. When they questioned the concierge of the building, she too denied ever seeing Annette or Josset.

'Doesn't Madame Malletier often receive young women?'

'Before, when she read the cards, she'd have both old and young, and even a few gentlemen, who you wouldn't think would go in for that sort of thing, but she hasn't been doing that for a while now.'

This was all fairly predictable. What wasn't so predictable was the attitude of Annette when Maigret called her into Quai des Orfèvres. The first question was blunt and to the point:

'How many weeks pregnant were you when you visited Madame Malletier in Rue Lepic?'

Didn't she know how to lie? Was she taken by surprise? Did she not realize the consequences of her answer?

She blushed, looked around as if seeking help and gave Lapointe, who was again taking everything down in shorthand, a worried look.

'I suppose I have to answer that?'

'That would be best.'

'Two months.'

'Who gave you the address in Rue Lepic?'

Maigret was a little irritated, for no good reason except perhaps that he thought she had given in a bit too easily. The concierge had played the game. The old abortionist too, of course, though she had every reason to do so.

'Adrien.'

'You told him you were pregnant, and he talked about an abortion?'

'It didn't happen quite like that. I had been fretting for six weeks, and he was constantly asking me what was bothering me. Once he even accused me of falling out of love with him. One evening, I asked him whether he knew of a midwife or a doctor who would be willing to . . .'

'He didn't protest?'

'He was stunned. He asked me:

'"Are you sure?"

'I told him yes, that I'd be showing soon, and that we had to do something about it.'

'Did he know Madame Malletier?'

'No. I don't think so. He told me to wait a few days and not do anything until he had decided.'

'Decided what?'

'I don't know.'

Josset didn't have any children with his wife. Was he moved by the thought that Annette might give him a son or a daughter?

Maigret, to set his mind at rest, would have liked to question him on this point and one or two others, but Coméliau was taking care of all the interrogations from now on, and he didn't see things from the same point of view.

'Do you think he was tempted to make you keep the baby?'

'I don't know.'

'Did he talk to you about it?'

'For a week he was more caring, paid me more attention.'

'Wasn't he normally caring?'

'He was kind, loving, but that's not the same thing.'

'Do you think he talked to his wife about it?'

She gave a start.

'His wife!'

It was as if she was afraid of Christine, even though she was dead.

'Surely he wouldn't have done that.'

'Why not?'

'I don't know . . . A man doesn't tell his wife he is expecting a child by another woman.'

'Was he scared of her?'

'He didn't hide from her. When I advised him to be careful, to not broadcast our relationship, for example, by being seen in restaurants, he told me she was in the picture and wouldn't do anything to him.'

'Did you believe him?'

'Not totally. It didn't seem possible to me.'

'Did you ever meet Christine Josset?'

'Several times.'

'Where?'

'At the office.'

'You mean in her husband's office?'

'Yes. I worked there too. When she came to Avenue Marceau . . .'

'Did she drop by often?'

'Two or three times a month.'

'To see her husband, to pick him up?'

'No. Mainly to see Monsieur Jules. She was chair of the board.'

'Was she actively involved in the business?'

'Not actively. She kept in touch, asked to see the accounts, to have certain things explained to her.'

It was a side of Christine that no one had talked about.

'I suppose she was curious about you?'

'In the beginning, yes. The very first time, she looked me over from head to toe, shrugged her shoulders and said to her husband:

'"Not bad . . ."'

'Did she already know?'

'Adrien had filled her in.'

'Did she ever talk to you one-to-one? Did you get the impression she was afraid of you?'

'Of me? Why would she be afraid of me?'

'If her husband had told her you were expecting a baby.'

'That would have made a difference, of course. But I would never have allowed him to tell her. Not just because of her, but because of others too.'

'Your colleagues?'

'Everyone. Also my father.'

'What happened at the end of the week?'

'One morning, in the office, before we opened the mail, he whispered to me quickly:

'"I've got an address. We have an appointment for this evening."

'That evening, as we left the office, he didn't drive me straight back to Rue Caulaincourt. He left the car at Boulevard de Clichy as a precaution, and we went on foot to Rue Lepic.'

'You weren't tempted to change your mind?'

'The old woman frightened me, but I had made my decision.'

'And him?'

'After a minute or two, he went out into the street to wait for me.'

Maigret passed on his report to Coméliau, as required. Was there then a leak from the magistrate's chambers? Coméliau wasn't the type to disseminate information of this nature. Was Lenain, who had been informed in a professional capacity, the one who was indiscreet? But publicity of this type was not in his client's interests, and although he committed many blunders, that surely wasn't one of them.

Most likely the person who had written the anonymous letter, annoyed that nothing had come of it, had taken the story to the papers, who conducted their own investigation.

Madame Malletier, who still denied everything, had been arrested, and the story was once again splashed over all the front pages.

Coméliau had been obliged to arrest the young woman too, but he later released her on bail.

JOSSET ACCUSED OF A SECOND CRIME ALONG
WITH HIS MISTRESS

When Annette was mentioned it was always in terms of pity; the full responsibility was laid at the door of her lover.

From one day to the next a palpable climate of hatred built up around him. Even those who had been his closest friends were reluctant to talk about him and tended to play down their relationship with him.

'I knew him like everyone else . . . It was Christine I was really friends with . . . An extraordinary woman!'

She showed extraordinary vitality, certainly. But what happened afterwards?

'She deserved better than him.'

When pushed, they were unable to say exactly what she

deserved. As far as anyone could tell, she was made to lead her own life, according to her own rules.

'For a while he had been her great love. No one knew why, since Josset was no Don Juan. Besides, he was a bit of a weakling.'

It seemed to cross no one's mind that Christine was more than capable of crushing this weakling.

'Didn't she love him any more?'

'They lived more and more separate lives. Especially after he fell for that typist.'

'Did it cause her pain?'

'It was difficult to tell exactly what Christine was feeling. She played her cards close to her chest.'

'Even when it came to lovers?'

They would give Maigret a look of reproach, as if he wasn't playing the game by the rules.

'She liked to help young people, didn't she?'

'She went to lots of arts events.'

'She took a few under her wing, as they say?'

'She helped young artists now and then.'

'Could you give me an example?'

'It's not easy. She was tactful enough not to make a big deal about it. She once, I recall, helped a young painter, particularly by bringing friends and journalists she knew along to his debut exhibition.'

'His name?'

'I can't remember . . . An Italian, I think.'

'Is that all?'

As time went on, the reticence became more and more concerted.

Maître Lenain, for his part, having rashly dropped his 'bombshell', was now trying to draw up a list of the so-called protégés whose existence he had so publicly proclaimed. Maigret didn't realize that he was being aided by a private detective agency run by one of his former inspectors. They had a freer rein than the Police Judiciaire and didn't have Coméliau on their backs all the time.

In spite of this he didn't turn up anything specific. He telephoned Maigret to tell him about a certain Daunard, a former hotel doorman from Deauville, who was now a singer in Saint-Germain-des-Prés.

Although he wasn't yet known to the wider public, he was starting to appear in cabarets on the Right Bank and was soon to make his music hall debut at the Bobino.

Maigret went to see him at his hotel room in Rue de Ponthieu. He was a tall, well-built young man, rough around the edges and a bit macho, like certain young American film stars. It was two o'clock in the afternoon, and he was still in crumpled pyjamas when he opened his door to Maigret. There was a woman entangled in his bedsheets, visible only by her blonde hair.

'Maigret, yeah?'

He had been anticipating this visit. He lit a cigarette and adopted the pose of a movie hard man.

'I could refuse to let you in unless you have a warrant. Do you?'

'No.'

'Then you should call me into your office.'

Maigret was in no mood to discuss the legal niceties.

'I should warn you I've got nothing to say.'

'Did you know Christine Josset?'

'So what? There are thousands of people in Paris who knew her.'

'Did you know her intimately?'

'One, that's none of your business. Two, if you look hard enough, you'll find dozens of young men who have slept with her. And when I say dozens . . .'

'When was the last time you saw her?'

'A good year ago. And if you are making out that she was the one who launched my career, you're wrong. When I was back in Deauville the owner of a club in Saint-Germain spotted me and gave me his card. He told me to come and look him up in Paris.'

The woman in his bed pulled the sheet down a few centimetres so that she could take a squint at what was going on.

'Don't worry, honey. I've got nothing to fear from these gentlemen. I can prove that on the night that Madame Christine was stiffed, I was down in Marseille. You'll even find my name in large letters on the poster at the Miramar.'

'Did you know any of the others?'

'Which others?'

'Other friends of Madame Josset's.'

'What, do you think we were some sort of club? We should have worn a badge or something, then, shouldn't we?'

He was terribly pleased with himself. His girlfriend was shaking with laughter under the sheet.

'Anything else I can do for you? If you don't mind, I have better things to do. That's right, isn't it, honey?'

There were surely others of the same type, or different, who evidently didn't want to make themselves known. The painter who was mentioned now lived in Brittany, where he painted seascapes, and there was nothing to suggest that he had come to Paris at the time of the murder.

A separate line of inquiry involving taxi-drivers had not thrown up anything either. Yet it is unusual, given enough time, not to find the driver who had done a particular trip.

Several inspectors had divided up the companies, the taxi stands and the owner-drivers between them.

They asked all of them if they had dropped off anyone in Rue Lopert on the evening of the crime, but that drew a blank. All they found out was that a couple who lived three doors down from the Jossets had taken a taxi home from the theatre and had arrived just before midnight.

Neither the driver nor the couple could remember seeing any lights in the glass house at that time.

There was one slight benefit of the taxi being there at that time, and that was that the old man, who claimed that he hadn't missed any of the comings and goings in the street, had failed to mention this particular car. Yet the car had parked there for two or three minutes, with its engine running, because the passenger didn't have enough change and had to go into the house to get some more money.

They had shown Martin Duché's photo to thousands of drivers, especially those who usually parked in the Caulaincourt area. They had all seen it in the newspapers. According to Annette, her father had left around 9.30 in the evening. He apparently hadn't returned to his hotel near Gare d'Austerlitz before midnight; later, the night clerk couldn't remember seeing him come back in at all.

What had the head clerk from Fontenay-le-Comte been doing all this time?

Here they drew a complete blank. None of the drivers could recall picking him up, even though he had a very distinctive face and figure.

Might he have tried to see Josset again, to ask him for an explanation, and to repeat the promise he had made?

Annette had admitted that he wasn't in his normal state of mind. Normally abstemious, he had been drinking heavily.

Even if the scene in Rue Caulaincourt had ended peacefully and in apparent agreement, it would have shaken him nonetheless.

Yet it seemed that no taxi had taken him to Rue Lopert, or indeed anywhere else.

No one had noticed him in the Métro station either, but given the volume of people passing through, that proved nothing.

Then there were the buses, where he could have equally passed unnoticed.

Was he the sort of person who would sneak inside Josset's house? Wouldn't he have rung the bell? Did he find the door open?

And is it conceivable that, in a place he didn't know, he could have crossed the living room in the dark, gone upstairs and entered Christine's room?

The murderer, assuming it wasn't the husband, had

worn gloves. Or else he had brought with him a weapon solid enough to inflict the wounds that Doctor Paul had described, or used the commando knife that was in Adrien's room.

But who, apart from people familiar to the couple, would know that that dagger was there? Then it would have to be admitted that, having committed the crime, the unknown murderer had cleaned the weapon, leaving no trace on any cloth, as Josset had not seen any blood on the knife.

The public were well aware of these things that didn't add up, as the journalists were very clever in dissecting all the possible hypotheses in the minutest detail. One had even published an article with the arguments for and the arguments against in two facing columns.

Maigret went to Avenue Marceau for the first time, to the turn-of-the-century town-house that had been converted into offices.

Apart from the switchboard and a small room where visitors left their cards and filled out a short form, the ground floor, with its panelled walls and moulded ceilings, was only used as a showroom.

The various products of Josset et Virieu were exhibited in glass cases, and there were medical diagrams and doctors' certificates in expensive frames. Finally, laid out on huge oak tables were a number of medical publications that helped to sell the firm's products.

It was Monsieur Jules that Maigret had come to see on this occasion. He had already found out that Jules was not his first name but his surname, so people didn't call him that out of familiarity.

A bright, almost empty room where two typists worked separated his office from that of Josset, which was the biggest in the firm, with tall windows overlooking the trees along the avenue.

Monsieur Jules was a man of sixty-five, with bushy eyebrows and dark hairs protruding from his nostrils and ears. He reminded Maigret of Martin Duché, only less docile. Like him, he was the very epitome of the faithful servant.

In fact, he was in the firm long before Josset came along, when old Virieu was still around, and although his job title was officially head of personnel, he also had oversight of other departments too.

Maigret wanted to talk to him about Christine.

'Don't trouble yourself, Monsieur Jules. I'm just passing through and, to be honest, I'm not even sure what it is I want to ask you. I just happened to find out that Madame Josset is the chair of your board.'

'That's right.'

'Is it just an honorary title or did she take an active interest in the running of the company?'

He could already sense the reticence he had encountered everywhere else. Isn't it precisely to head this off that it is so important in a criminal investigation to move quickly?

Madame Maigret knew that as well as anyone, as she often saw her husband come home in the early hours of the morning, that is if he wasn't out for several nights in a row.

When people read the papers they form instant

opinions and even when they think they are being sincere and honest, they tend to distort the truth.

'She really got involved in the business. She had a substantial stake in it, after all.'

'One-third of the capital, unless I am mistaken?'

'A third of the shares, yes, with another third staying in the hands of Monsieur Virieu and the other third for the last few years in the possession of her husband.'

'I've been told that she came to see you two or three times a month.'

'Not as regularly as that. She dropped by from time to time, not just to see me but also to see the chief executive and sometimes the head of accounts.'

'Did she know what was what?'

'She had a very good head for business. She speculated on the Stock Exchange on her own account, and I don't mind saying she made some tidy profits.'

'In your opinion, did she have doubts about her husband's way of running the business?'

'Not just about her husband in particular, but everyone.'

'Did her attitude make enemies?'

'Everyone has enemies.'

'Did she have any in this firm? Did she have to take measures against any individuals?'

Monsieur Jules scratched his nose, a malicious look in his eye, not the slightest bit embarrassed but somewhat hesitant.

'Have you studied how large companies organize themselves and their staff, inspector? As long as there are competing personal interests and departments working to different agendas, it's inevitable that cliques form.'

The same was true of Quai des Orfèvres, as Maigret knew only too well.

'Were there cliques here in this firm?'

'Probably still are.'

'May I ask you which one you belonged to?'

Monsieur Jules frowned, became more sombre and stared at his pigskin desk accoutrements.

'I was completely devoted to Madame Josset,' he said finally, carefully weighing his words.

'And her husband?'

At that, he got up and went to check that no one was listening behind the door.

8. Madame Maigret's Coq au Vin

It was the Maigrets' turn to host their friends at Boulevard Richard-Lenoir, and Madame Maigret had been cooking all day amid a symphony of various noises, for the season of wide-open windows had begun, and the life of Paris blew into the apartments on the currents of air.

Alice hadn't come along, and it was her mother, this time, who listened out for the telephone, because at any moment they were expecting the young woman to be rushed into the clinic to give birth.

Once dinner was over, the table cleared and coffee served, Maigret offered the doctor a cigar, while the two women whispered together in a corner, and Madame Pardon was heard to say:

'I really don't know how you do it.'

She was talking about the coq au vin they had had for dinner. She went on:

'There is that subtle aftertaste which really sets it apart, I can't quite identify what it is.'

'It's actually quite simple. I presume you normally add a dash of cognac at the last moment?'

'Cognac, armagnac, whatever I have to hand.'

'Well, I know it's not orthodox, but I use Alsatian plum brandy. That's my secret.'

During dinner, Maigret had been in a good mood.

'Busy?' Pardon asked him.

'Very.'

Which was true, but it was fun work.

'I'm living in the middle of a circus!'

For a while there had been a series of burglaries that could only have been committed by a professional acrobat, probably a male or female contortionist, and so Maigret and his colleagues had been spending their days from morning to night in the world of the circus and the music hall, and had seen the most extraordinary array of people passing through Quai des Orfèvres.

They were dealing with a new arrival who used new methods, which happens more rarely than you might think. So routines had to be relearned from scratch, and the Crime Squad was a hotbed of excitement.

'Last month you didn't have time to finish your story about the Josset case,' Doctor Pardon murmured, once he had settled into his chair with a drink by his side.

He never had more than one, but he drank it in small sips, swilling it round his mouth so as to better appreciate the bouquet.

At the mention of the murder in Rue Lopert, a different expression came over the inspector's face.

'I can't remember where I got to . . . From the start I had guessed that Coméliau wouldn't give me the chance to see Josset again, and that's how it turned out. He was so possessive of him you might almost say he was jealous.

'The case was built within the four walls of his chambers, and the police didn't know anything more about it than what was printed in the papers.

'For nearly two months, ten of my men, sometimes more, were bogged down in fact-checking.

'Our investigation worked on different levels simultaneously. Firstly, on a purely technical level, we reconstructed the movements of each person on the night of the crime, searched the house in Rue Lopert twenty times over, hoping to find a clue that we had missed before, including the famous commando knife.

'I don't know how many times I questioned the two servants, the tradesmen, the neighbours. And our task was complicated by the flow of letters, both anonymous and signed, but mainly anonymous, which we couldn't ignore.

'It always happens when a case stirs up public opinion.

'Cranks, crackpots, people who have had a grudge against their neighbour for years or simply people who think they know something – they all get in touch with the police, who have then to separate the fact from the fiction.

'I went to Fontenay-le-Comte in secret, almost under false pretences, but found nothing, as I think I already told you.

'You see, Pardon, once a crime is committed, nothing is straightforward any more. There are ten or maybe twenty people whose actions may have seemed perfectly normal a few hours earlier but now have to be scrutinized in a more suspicious light.

'*Everything is possible!*

'No hypothesis can be ruled out as ridiculous. Nor is there any infallible method for being sure of the witnesses' good faith or powers of recall.

'The public follows its gut instinct, driven by emotion and only the most elementary reasoning.

'As for us, we have the duty to doubt everything, to look everywhere, to consider every possible explanation.

'So, Rue Lopert on the one hand, Avenue Marceau on the other.

'I knew nothing about the pharmaceutical industry, so I had to learn how this business worked. With all its laboratories and more than 300 staff.

'And, based on a few conversations, what to make of Monsieur Jules and the way his mind operated?

'And he wasn't the only one who played a significant role in Avenue Marceau. There was Virieu, the son of the firm's founder, then the heads of the various departments, the technical advisers, doctors, pharmacists, chemists . . .

'All these people divided into two main camps, which for the sake of argument we might call the ancients and the moderns. The former thought that the company should concentrate on prescription drugs only; the latter wanted to produce lucrative products that could be marketed through publicity campaigns in the papers and on the radio.'

Pardon murmured:

'I'm not unfamiliar with that debate.'

'It seems that Josset had a natural inclination towards the former, but let himself be pushed against his will into the second category.

'Though not without putting up a struggle.'

'What about his wife?'

'She was the leader of the moderns. Under pressure from her, a sales director had been fired two months earlier, a valued employee who had good links with their medical clients and was a sworn enemy of all-purpose medicines.

'All this created a climate of intrigue, suspicion and probably mutual loathing at Avenue Marceau and in Saint-Mandé . . . But that didn't get me anywhere.

'We couldn't examine every aspect in depth at the same time. Mostly our officers are engaged in existing case-work, even when something sensational comes along.

'I've never felt our inherent weakness so keenly. At a time when we needed to understand the lives of a dozen, maybe as many as thirty, individuals about whom we knew nothing the day before, I had only a handful of men at my disposal.

'They were being asked to probe into areas with which they weren't familiar and, in a ridiculously short space of time, form an opinion.

'But in court the words of a witness, a concierge, a taxi-driver, a neighbour, a man in the street might have more weight than all the sworn testimonies and denials of the accused.

'For two months I toiled with an acute sense of my own impotence, yet I carried on, hoping against hope for a miracle.

'Adrien Josset continued to profess his innocence, despite being increasingly presumed guilty. His lawyer continued to make reckless statements to the press.

'I counted fifty-three anonymous letters, which led us to every corner of Paris and its suburbs. We even had to send letters of request outside of Paris.

'Some people had thought they had seen Martin Duché

in Auteuil during the night, and there was even a female vagrant near Pont Mirabeau who claimed that Annette's father had made drunken advances to her.

'Others named young men they considered to be Christine Josset's protégés.

'We followed every lead, even the unlikely ones, and each evening I sent a report to Coméliau, who flicked through it with a shrug of his shoulders.

'One of the young men who were pointed out to us was called Popaul. The anonymous letter said:

'"You will find him at the Bar de la Lune, Rue de Charonne, where everyone knows him, but they won't say a thing because they all have something to hide."

'The writer of the letter provided details and said that Christine Josset liked slumming it and that she had met Popaul on several occasions in a rented room near Canal Saint-Martin.

'"She had bought him a 4CV, but that didn't prevent Popaul from beating her on numerous occasions and extorting money from her."'

Maigret went himself to Rue de Charonne, and the bistro mentioned in the letter was indeed a den of villains who made themselves scarce when he turned up. He questioned the owner, the waitress and then, in the following days, the regulars, whom he had some difficulty pinning down.

'Popaul? Never heard of him.'

The innocence was rather forced. If they were to be believed, no one knew this Popaul, and he would have no more joy asking in the boarding houses along the canal.

At the car licensing centre they hadn't found any useful

information. Several recent owners of 4CVs had the name Paul. They tracked down a few, but four or five had left Paris.

As for Christine's friends, they all maintained the same polite silence. Christine was a charming woman, a *sweetheart*, a *darling*, a *remarkable woman*.

Madame Maigret had taken Madame Pardon into the kitchen to show her God knows what, then the two women, in order to leave the men in peace, had settled down in the dining room. Maigret, who had removed his jacket, was smoking a meerschaum pipe he only ever used at home.

'The Grand Jury was appointed, and so our work was officially over. We were busy with other cases during the summer. The newspapers announced that Josset had suffered from depression and had been transferred to the hospital at the Santé, where he was being treated for a stomach ulcer.

'That raised a few smiles, since it was something of a tradition for the better class of prisoner to fall ill as soon as they got put in jail.

'When, after the summer recess, he appeared on the witness stand, he had clearly lost twenty kilos and was not the man he once was. His clothes hung off his thin frame, his eyes were sunken in their sockets, and for all his lawyer put on a show to both witnesses and the public, he seemed somewhat indifferent to what was going on around him.

'I didn't hear the judge's questioning of the accused, nor the testimony of Coméliau and the chief inspector from Auteuil, who were the first ones called to give evidence, because I was still in the witness room. Sitting there with me, among others, were the concierge from Rue Caulaincourt, wearing a red hat, looking very smug and sure of herself, and Monsieur Lalinde, the former colonial administrator, whose evidence was the most damning, and who seemed in a bad way. I thought he too had lost weight. He seemed to have something on his mind, and it made me wonder whether he was about to alter his earlier statement in court.

'For better or worse, I added my brick to the edifice so carefully constructed by the prosecution.

'I was just an instrument. I could only say what I had seen, what I had heard. No one asked for my opinion.

'I spent the rest of those two days in the courtroom. Lalinde didn't retract his statement, didn't change a single word of what he had already said.

'During the recesses, I heard members of the public talking in the corridors, and it was clear that no one was in any doubt about Josset's guilt.

'Annette appeared on the witness stand, which caused a commotion, as whole rows of people stood up to get a better look, and the judge threatened to clear the court.

'She was asked detailed questions, rather leading in the way they were put, particularly about the abortion.

'"Was it Josset who took you to see Madame Malletier in Rue Lepic?"

'"Yes, Your Honour."

'"Please turn and face the jury . . ."

'She wanted to add something, but they had already moved on to the next question.'

Several times, Maigret had the impression that she was trying to make a more subtle point, but no one was interested. Wasn't it she, for example, who, when she told her lover that she was pregnant, asked him if he knew an abortionist?

'And so it went on,' Maigret told Pardon.

Sitting on the public benches, he couldn't keep still. He was constantly tempted to raise his hand and intervene.

'In two days, barely a dozen hours in total, including the reading of the charge and the summing-up by both prosecutor and counsel, they claimed to be able to summarize, to a group of men who had previously known nothing, a whole life, describe not just one person's character but several, as they also discussed Christine, Annette, her father and other secondary players.

'It was hot in the courtroom, as we were having a superb Indian summer that year. Josset spotted me. On several occasions our eyes met, but it was only towards the end of the first day that he seemed to recognize me and gave me a slight smile.

'Did he realize that I had doubts, that this case gave me an uneasy feeling, that I was dissatisfied with my own and others' performance and that, because of him, I had begun to feel disgusted by my profession?

'I don't know. Most of the time he seemed immersed in an apathy that many court reporters interpreted as contempt. Since he had taken a certain care over his appearance, they spoke of his vanity, and cleverly highlighted other examples of it in his work life and even in his childhood and youth

'The attorney general, who was conducting the prosecution himself, also emphasized his vanity:

'"A vain weakling . . ."

'Maître Lenain's rhetorical sallies did nothing to change the mood of the courtroom; quite the opposite, in fact!

'When the jury retired to consider its verdict, I knew already the answer to the first question – did Josset kill his wife? – would be "yes", and probably unanimous.

'I had hoped the answer to the second one – concerning premeditation – would be negative by a narrow margin. And as for attenuating circumstances . . .

'There were people eating sandwiches, women passing round sweets. The reporters reckoned they had just enough time to nip out for a drink in the bar.

'It was quite late when the jury returned with their verdict. The president of the jury, an ironmonger from the sixth arrondissement, held a piece of paper in his trembling hand.

'"On the first question: yes."

'"On the second question: yes."

'"On the third question: no."

'Josset was found guilty of the premeditated murder of his wife and refused the benefit of any attenuating circumstances.

'I saw him as the shock hit him. He turned pale, looked surprised; he couldn't believe his ears at first. He waved his arms around, as if struggling, then he suddenly became calm and turned to the public and, with one of the most tragic expressions I have ever seen in my life, said in a firm voice:

'"I am innocent."

'There were a few boos. One woman fainted. The stewards rushed into the courtroom.

'In the blink of an eye, Josset was whisked away. One month later the press announced that the President of the Republic had turned down his appeal for clemency.

'No one bothered with him any more. Another case had captured the public's imagination, a sex scandal in which each day brought some new salacious revelation, and Josset's execution, when it came, was given no more than a few lines on page five of the newspapers.'

There was a silence. Pardon stubbed out his cigar in the ashtray while Maigret filled a fresh pipe, and the women's voices could be heard from the other room.

'Do you believe he was innocent?'

'Twenty years ago, when I was still new to the force, I might have said "yes" without hesitation. Since then, I've learned that anything, no matter how unlikely, is possible.

'Two years after the trial I had a lowlife in my office who was suspected of involvement in the white slave trade. It wasn't the first time he'd had dealings with us. He was one of our regular customers.

'His identity card said he was a navigator, and in fact he did make regular crossings to South and Central America on board cargo ships, though he spent most of his time in Paris.

'With people like him it's different. You're on familiar territory.

'Sometimes we do deals.

'At one point, he squinted at me out of the corner of his eye and murmured:

'"What if I have something valuable to sell?"

'"Like what?"

'"A piece of information I think you'll find interesting."

'"Concerning what?"

'"The Josset case."

'"That was concluded a long time ago."

'"That's not necessarily a reason . . ."

'In return, he asked me to lay off his girlfriend, with whom he seemed genuinely in love. I promised to go easy on her.

'"On my last voyage, to Venezuela, I met a guy called Popaul. He used to hang around Bastille a lot."

'"Rue de Charonne?"

'"Maybe. He seemed to be down on his luck, so I bought him a few drinks. Around three or four in the morning, when he'd polished off a half-bottle of tequila and was drunk, he started talking: 'The gang leaders around here don't think I'm a hard case. Even when I tell them I slashed a woman in Paris they don't believe me. Even less when I tell them she was a rich woman and she was crazy about me. But it's true, and I'll always regret how stupid I was. Only, I just can't stand being treated in that way, and she shouldn't have pushed me so far. Have you heard about the Josset case?'"'

Maigret stopped talking. He removed his pipe from his mouth.

After a silence that seemed to go on for a long time, he added almost with regret:

'My customer couldn't tell me anything else. This so-called Popaul – if there really was a Popaul, people sometimes have vivid imaginations – carried on drinking and eventually fell asleep. The next day he claimed he couldn't remember a thing . . .'

'Did you contact the Venezuelan police?'

'Unofficially, as there was the matter of *res judicata*. Over there they have a number of French people who have every reason not to return home, including some ex-convicts. In response to my request I received an official letter asking me to provide fuller details concerning his identity.

'Does this Popaul exist? And was his male ego and his image of himself as a tough guy so bruised by the fact that she treated him the way men treat girls they pick up in the street that he took his revenge on her?

'I have no way of knowing.'

He got up and went to the window, as if to clear his head.

Pardon was watching the telephone almost without thinking, so Maigret asked him:

'Tell me, what happened to the little Polish tailor's family?'

It was the doctor's turn to shrug.

'Three days ago I was called out to Rue Popincourt, because one of the children had measles, and I found that the wife was already living with a North African. She seemed a little embarrassed and she said:

'"It's for the kids, you see . . . ?"'